MW00941704

Happy Haunting!

A Spirited Manor

by Kate Danley

Kate Danley
2022

THE O'HARE HOUSE MYSTERY SERIES

Want the latest news on Kate Danley books and releases?
Sign up for her newsletter at
www.katedanley.com/subscribe.html

This is a work of fiction. All of the characters, organizations, and events portrayed in this novel are either products of the author's imagination or are used fictitiously.

FIRST EDITION - A SPIRITED Manor. Copyright © 2013 Kate Danley. All rights reserved.

Second Edition - A Spirited Manor. Copyright © 2017 Kate Danley.

First Printing

Cover Art Image by Book Art Media

Second Printing

Cover Art by Lou Harper

Third Printing

Cover Art by Self Pub Book Covers FrinaArt

Fourth Printing

Cover Art by Mariah Sinclair | www.mariahsinclair.com

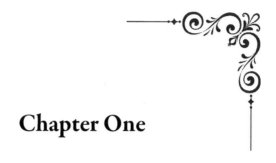

Chapter One

The murmur of the city and the gentle clip-clop of the horse drifted inside the dark hansom cab as it rocked back and forth. Clara looked down at her gloved hands. The black leather encasing her fingers matched the black crepe of her skirt. The only color came from her fiery-red hair, but she kept it pulled back as tightly as she could, hiding it beneath her black bonnet in the hope the world would leave her alone. In a few moments, she knew the carriage would stop, and when it did, she would have to begin her new life.

She felt like her heartbeat had been replaced by the hollow sound of the horse's hooves echoing upon the cobblestones.

It had been six months since her husband passed away, six months of being haunted by Thomas's memory. He had died without warning. He went into the office one day, rested his head upon his desk, and when his partner stopped to ask him if anything was the matter, Thomas was gone. His heart just stopped, and when it did, it seemed to stop hers, too. She was left with nothing but a terrible emptiness in her chest, the aching memory of what once lived there.

Christmas... New Years... all of the excitement that 1890 should have brought... It was darkness. Every brick and tile of their home reminded her of their time together. She expected to see him every time she turned the corner in every room and she could not take it anymore without going mad. She had to leave.

Today, she was moving into her own house. It would be hers, alone.

If not for the passage of the Women's Property Act only eight years earlier, she would have been destitute and on the street. Instead, she was able to sell their house and use the proceeds to buy the new building. She received a pension as his widow, so she knew she would be taken care of until the end of her days. Thinking back to the years that she and Thomas struggled with their finances, though, scrimping and saving every penny... She wiped away a tear that secreted its way onto her cheek. What use was all the comfort in the world when he was gone?

The cab turned the corner into the square. She gazed out the window. Her new home was at the far end of a pretty green park. When she bought it, she thought perhaps gazing upon the seasons as trees bloomed and birds were born might be something she could enjoy someday. But for now, it only reminded her that she had no one to share these tiny miracles with. They seemed something that must be endured.

The cab drew up in front of the row house and the driver stepped down to give her his hand. He took down her bags and set them beside her. She tipped him and then he climbed back aboard and drove off, leaving her alone on the street.

The house could be described as a charming two-story residence, matching smartly with its next door neighbors and the other homes lining the square. Its bricked face and black shutters harkened back to an earlier time. She'd purchased it for almost a song. Such a home should have been well beyond her means, but the previous owner, a Lord Horace Oroberg, had been just as anxious to get rid of it as she was to find a new place to live. A young woman had been found dead there some years before—some said murdered, others said suicide—but most certainly she died within its walls, which caused it to be difficult to sell.

Perhaps Clara should have been disturbed by the home's checkered past, but instead, she felt a kinship. Here was a lovely house, ruined by no fault of its own, and yet the world could no longer look on it the same. It felt as if this home needed her almost as much as she needed it.

The door opened, revealing a tall gentleman dressed impeccably in coat and tails. He was older, his peppered hair slicked neatly across his balding pate. Behind him emerged an older woman, almost his female twin, in a black dress and apron.

"Welcome, Mrs. O'Hare," the butler said, bowing politely. "We are so glad to see you have arrived." He walked swiftly, helping before Clara could even respond. "May I take your bags? Mrs. Nan can get you settled and dressed for dinner."

Mrs. Nan smiled, welcoming her in.

"Quite kind of you, Mr. Willard," Clara replied as Mr. Willard gathered her things. "That would be lovely."

Mr. Willard let it slip when she first came to look at the house that he and Mrs. Nan had been left behind by Lord Oroberg and were in need of employment. Though Clara truly only needed a housekeeper, she felt it would be a great unkindness to send Mr. Willard onto the street after so many years of loyal service. So upon transfer of ownership, Clara engaged them both.

Clara stepped through the door with Mr. Willard behind her. She stood for a moment, allowing him to pass and take her things up to her room. She removed her hat and passed it to Mrs. Nan. "I shall be upstairs in just a moment. I would like a few minutes by myself."

Mrs. Nan gave a nod and followed Mr. Willard to Clara's room.

Clara stood in the foyer, upon the white and black octagon tile, and let the place sink into her. Home. This strange building with all its secrets was to be her home. To the left was a paneled study, its library shelves empty. She thought of how Thomas would have delighted in filling them with books of mathematics and poetry. She could almost envision him sitting at the desk, but she stopped herself. She did not need to fill this home with ghosts. To her right was the parlor. Its sliding doors were open. The walls were painted a light green instead of the dark, busy wallpaper which was so popular nowadays. At the end of the hall would be the lonely dining room, where she would have to sit by herself tonight, served by strangers, as kind as they might be, and assume the role and duties of a lady of the house. She could almost weep.

She walked up the carpeted, walnut staircase to the room where Mrs. Nan waited. The staircase wall would be a perfect place to hang portraits of old family members or pastorals painted during a happy holiday. Clara had rid herself of all those things. Instead, she brought only the objects which held memories from before Thomas came into her life — ancient furniture owned by her grandparents, the tables and chairs she bought while attending school. But anything that bore his touch was gone. She hoped that, somehow, by purging her world of the things which brought on the memories, she could send away some of the pain, too. She did not yet know if it was of aid.

The staircase emptied into a windowless hallway. Gas lamps lit the way for her, their flickering light dancing with the darkness. The door to her room stood open at the end, ready to welcome her in. She had chosen a room in the back, in the quiet farthest from the street. There were several rooms on this floor. She would keep them for the guests that she would never invite.

She stepped inside and was pleased that it seemed like staying in a hotel, into someone else's life. Lord Oroberg left the furnishings and she bought them with the house. There was a large clothes cupboard, a four-poster bed, a few chairs, a full length mirror, and a dressing table. Nothing of her own beyond the clothes in her bags, which had been chosen new since the funeral. She would never need anything other than their black shapes.

"Can I help you change for dinner, ma'am?" asked Mrs. Nan in her soft, compassionate voice. "Get you out of those dusty clothes and into something nice and fresh?"

"That would be lovely. Thank you," she replied.

She stood like a child as Mrs. Nan's wrinkled fingers expertly made their way over the buttons running down the back of her gown. The dress fell stiffly to the floor and Clara stepped out of it.

"Would you like to sit down with me tomorrow and we can go through the week's menu and schedule?"

Clara tried to smile, to return this woman's kindness instead of retreating into the detachment where she more comfortably lived. "I trust your household knowledge to be far superior to mine. Whatever you did for the family before will be far better than anything I can devise."

"Such a dear family," Mrs. Nan said. She clucked her tongue as she hung up Clara's dress. "Such a tragedy."

Clara felt her interest raise its head, and for once, the words were not mechanical. "I heard someone died in this house. Do you know what happened?"

Mrs. Nan raised Clara's evening dress and helped her climb inside. "Aye, I know well enough. 'Twas a member of the house staff, too. I knew her since she was a wee little child. Found dead in her rooms almost fifteen years ago. Some say she turned her hand upon herself, but I never heard of such nonsense. It was murder, plain and clear. And the police not even batting an eye! So happy to walk away and declare the case was closed. We'll never know who did it. We'll never know of what evil infiltrated our walls." Mrs. Nan began fastening the buttons around Clara's neck. "Such a young thing. So much of life cut short. She never even knew love."

"Perhaps she was the lucky one," said Clara, buttoning her sleeves as Mrs. Nan continued her work down the back.

Mrs. Nan turned Clara around to face her. She took a moment, as if trying to decide whether to speak or not. Finally, motherly, she took Clara's hands in her own and grasped them tight. "I know from all this black you swathe yourself in, dear, that you lost someone close to your heart. I know it must feel like the world should end. But in the years to come, I promise the sun will rise upon a day where you are happy to have known him, grateful for the time you had together. I promise you."

Clara could not help it. Her throat tightened and she feared that her sadness would spill out before she could wrest it back in and hide it away.

But Mrs. Nan just smoothed back a loosened tendril of Clara's curly red hair and said, "Never feel like you need to hide those tears from me, duck. I've known my share of love and loss, and I know. I know..." Mrs. Nan brushed back a tear from her own eye. "Now... Mr. Willard should have the dinner on, if you're ready."

Clara nodded and followed after Mrs. Nan. She hoped that someday she would be grateful for her time with Thomas. She hoped someday that the housekeeper's words would come true. But right now, she would have given up knowing him at all if it meant she did not have to live with this broken heart.

Chapter Two

Dinner was quiet. Mr. Willard served Clara with the polite deference of his station. She wished there was not a wall between them almost as much as she was glad she had societal excuses not to make idle chat. Navigating the world of the living with its niceties and inane ramblings left her exhausted, when once upon a time it was what she lived for. Before Thomas's passing, she was gladly the center of attention at any get-together. He had reveled in her spirit, watched her admiringly from across the room as her wit caused peals of laughter. He spoke often and proudly of the way she made others feel welcome with just a word and a touch. Now she felt old and useless, and nothing but hollow sounds left her mouth.

She could tell that Mrs. Nan had worked hard to make the meal, and she ate as much as she could to seem grateful for the effort, but was only too happy when she could excuse herself from the table and make her way upstairs to her bedchambers where she could say goodbye to another day. She supposed that if anyone were to listen to her thoughts, they would seem morbid, they would probably throw her in an asylum and toss away the key, but she looked forward to the night. She looked forward to placing her head upon her pillow and closing her eyes, knowing that as soon as she fell asleep, she had one less day to live, and was one day closer to being reunited with Thomas. The only thing that got her through living was knowing the day would come when she would not have to do it anymore. She would suffer through until the end and welcome it with open arms when it arrived. Her only prayer now consisted of four words: Let it be soon.

Mrs. Nan helped her into her white cotton gown and extinguished the gas lamps in the room. Clara put her head upon her pillow, and as soon as the door closed, let the tears fall as they had every night for six months. Sometimes she felt as if Thomas were so close, he was almost in the room with her. But he was not here. She tried so hard to chase every shadow of him away and yet, as she lay there in the darkness, she could not help the memories of him which filled her mind. She could not keep away the pain.

She closed her eyes and hoped for dreams of reunion, of warmth and comfort. Too many nights passed with darkness, with confusing images of chasing something down a dark hallway and never being able to find it, whatever it was.

But tonight, as she dreamt of running down that same dark hallway, she thought she heard someone softly whispering her name, someone calling out, "Clara."

It was enough to make her open her eyes and sit up in bed.

The room was frigid, so cold that Clara could see her breath before her face. She shivered and clutched the bedcover to her chin. She was not sure what was real and what was not. She could see the glowing embers in the grate, and yet, the room felt like February. The curtains blew gently and the moon bathed everything in an unearthly blue light. She leapt out of bed, sure that somehow one of the windows must have come open. But they were all closed and locked.

And then the moonlight disappeared, and with it, the heat returned. Clara looked around, becoming more and more aware of her surroundings. She pinched herself and was reassured of her reality. It had all been a dream, some strange night terror. Sleep walking was almost a nightly occurrence in the weeks after Thomas's death, but she thought she had moved on. She tried to comfort herself with the fact she was now awake and everything was fine, but she was filled with a strange sense of foreboding. She looked over to the window and touched it, as if to convince herself that it was closed.

She walked back over to the bed and climbed beneath the covers. There were no strong arms there to soothe her, to tell her she was safe and all she needed to do was close her eyes and the morning would come. Though she tried to seek out sleep, it seemed to have decided that she would not get a second visit. Instead, Clara was left staring at the ceiling all night, sadly realizing that despite all her efforts, nothing had changed.

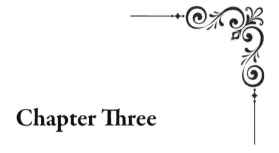

Chapter Three

"Did you sleep well, ma'am?" Mr. Willard asked.

Clara sat in the dining room. She tested the head of the tea Mr. Willard had just poured. Mrs. Nan made her a most excellent breakfast. Clara was sure it must have been to try and show her new mistress all that she was capable of. Clara wished that she were not so tired so that she could be more appreciative. She took a bite from her toast. "Unfortunately, no. I had the strangest dream," she replied, "and it kept me up the rest of the night."

"Really?" he said with polite sympathy.

"I dreamt someone called my name, and then that one of the windows was open. In this dream, my room was so frightfully cold, it felt like going into a winter snowstorm without a wrap. It seemed so real, I actually got out of bed to close the pane, but the window was closed."

Mr. Willard fumbled the tongs, and they clanked upon the platter. His face turned red in embarrassment. "Apologies."

"None needed, Mr. Willard."

He brought the plate over. "This house can become quite drafty at night," he said as she helped herself to some eggs. "I shall make sure that we heat your bed extra warm tonight."

"Oh, it is quite all right. I am afraid that since my late husband's death, sleep has not been my friend. The fact I rested at all is a sign of the comfort and safety you and Mrs. Nan have made me feel here."

She wondered how cruel his former employer had been, for just those few kind words made him practically beam with pride. He was quick to hide it, but she saw. He immediately seemed to want to prove her faith well-founded and fussed. "Still, it will not do at all. We shall make sure to send you to bed with warm milk tonight and see if we can't chase away those dreams."

"That would be lovely," Clara said. She pushed back from the table. "Please tell Mrs. Nan that breakfast was wonderful and she has set the bar quite high. Now, I feel the need for a bit of a stroll. If you will please excuse me."

"Of course, ma'am." Mr. Willard followed her to the door. From out of nowhere, he somehow had her hat, parasol, gloves, and purse in hand and ready. He passed them one-by-one to her as she put them on. "Shall we expect you home for lunch?"

Clara stared outdoors, unsure of her answer. She realized she had no place to be. No one to visit. No errands to run. All was taken care of, and she wondered if she should even go outside at all. It would be so much easier to close the shades and sit in the darkness. She looked over at Mr. Willard, and realized that she did not want such a kind and caring soul to see her in such weakness. Already she knew that he would not let her hide. He would take her gloomy spirit personally, as some sort of failing on his part, and that would not do at all. She managed a stiff smile, as if somehow she could cover the terror she felt about finding a way to pass all the hours ahead of her. "No...

no, I believe that I shall be out all day. I shall return tonight for dinner," she replied.

He gave her a bow. "Very well. We shall be sure to have something warm and delicious waiting for you by six o'clock."

She nodded. "Thank you, Mr. Willard."

And then she stepped out into the sunlight.

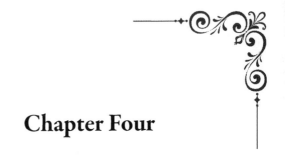

Chapter Four

The hours seemed to stretch inexorably before her, each moment ticking by painfully slow. Usually, she would just lie in bed, waiting for another day to pass. She had not even realized that it was spring. She wandered down to the public park, buying herself a bag of crumbs to feed to the ducks. They seemed appreciative and clamored about her until the bag was empty, and then were gone as quickly as they appeared. She watched as couples strolled and children played. She slipped through them like a ghost. None even acknowledged her presence. Her gown of black seemed a camouflage which hid her from joy-filled eyes. She tried to find interest in gazing upon the blooming tulips and daffodils. She wandered into the zoo, but the bears and tigers were sleeping in their cages. She sat upon a bench and realized that it was barely noon.

She left the park and walked along the boulevard, its wide lanes filled with trolley cars and hansom cabs. There were shops whose windows were filled with trinkets, but nothing which tempted her to go in. She was caught in a crowded clump of businessmen as the lunch hour struck and, uncaring, let herself be swept along. She could barely see over their shoulders, when suddenly, out of the corner of her eye, she saw a man hurry by.

"Thomas?" she whispered. She knew it could not be him, but this man's shape, his coloring, his carriage... for a moment she wondered if Thomas's death could have been all a terrible misunderstanding. She rushed to catch up, trying to push her way politely through the throng. But by the time she broke free, he was gone.

Her heart fell as she stood there, a passerby jostling her elbow. She lifted her eyes as she tried to force down the disappointment, and they fell upon the marquee for a vaudeville house. It seemed a godsend. For the cost of a single coin, she could sit quietly in a chair for as long as she wished with no one to trouble her. She would have a good answer when Mr. Willard or Mrs. Nan asked how she spent her day. Whether she was amused by the acts or not made no difference. She could escape, she could hide in the crowd, and be as alone as she wished in plain sight.

Gladly, she paid the booth and clutched her ticket. She walked into the lobby and purchased a paper cone filled with peanuts. She walked into the theater with its velvet seats and curtains. It was busy, but by no means full. She found a seat in the back and far from any other guests. She sat down, feeling as if she could breathe for the very first time all day.

The performers were talented, first a brother-and-sister duo who sang and danced their way across the stage. Then an acrobat troop that tumbled and juggled. A diva stepped into the limelight and sang a song of sorrow. Clara could tell the woman had no idea what it meant.

The master of ceremonies took the stage after the diva, clapping enthusiastically as he tried to rally the audience from their stupor. "And now, ladies and gentlemen, we ask that those faint of heart leave the premises. Our next act shall tear aside the veil of life and death, shall reveal to you the mysteries of the world beyond! Please join me in welcoming one of the most powerful mediums of our age, Wesley Lowenherz!"

A man stepped onto the stage. He was tall, with a square jaw and broad shoulders. He had auburn curly hair which extended into the longer sideburns that were all the rage in fashionable circles. Beyond that, Clara could not make out his face. The footlights threw strange shadows upon him and the greasepaint morphed his features. There was something about him, though. Something strange yet familiar. It was not his appearance, it was him. It made no sense, but Clara sat forward in her chair.

"Ladies and gentlemen," Wesley began. "I come before you to reunite you with loved ones passed. To answer your questions of life and death. I come not to bring pain, but to bring healing, to give hope to the hopeless and to let you know you are not alone." He lifted his forefingers to either side of his temples and closed his eyes.

Clara's heart caught in her throat. She knew what he was going to say before he said it, but sat paralyzed as the words came out.

"Is there someone here who has lost a loved one? A gentleman perhaps? I am sensing a letter. 'T'. A name that begins with 'T'?"

It was all that Clara could do to not leap from her seat, to beg him to tell her more. It was equally as impossible to keep from fleeing the theater, to run from this man who could see more than what a man should see. She did not want to share her loneliness and misery before a paying crowd, those who would dismiss a message from her Thomas as nothing but a charlatan's trick. And yet, if it was her Thomas, if it was her one opportunity to speak to him when he left her so all alone... She was frozen by fear and uncertainty.

"A gentleman whose name begins with a 'T'?"

She felt her hand beginning to raise, the ache to call out that yes, it was her, this message was for her, rose in her throat, but just as she summoned the courage, a woman close to the stage stood up. "Toby? Is it my Toby come to say hello to his old mum?"

The man held out his hand. "Indeed, Madame! Toby! Please, join me on the stage so that I may give you the message he has traveled from the grave to bring to you!"

Clara did not know whether the feeling which struck her heart was relief or terrible sadness. She clapped dutifully with the rest of the audience as the old woman toddled up the stairs. The rest of the act was a blur as Clara gathered her things, suddenly desperate to be away from there.

She rose from her seat and made her way to the aisle. Just as she was about to leave, Wesley held out his hands. "Wait! Another message has come!"

She turned and it seemed as if he were looking straight at her, even though she knew he could not see into the darkness of the audience beyond the haze of the footlights. Still, he seemed to almost lock eyes with her as he said, "There is a woman here tonight. You know who you are. And your loved one says, 'Do not fear to live and love again, for watching your sadness is worse than death. Do not die while you are still alive, my love.'"

And with that, Clara fled.

Chapter Five

She arrived home in a daze. She knew that Mr. Willard spoke with her, that Mrs. Nan prepared a lovely dinner, that somehow she was led up to her room and dressed for bed. Mrs. Nan ran a metal pan filled with coals over her sheets to make them toasty, and a warm glass of milk sat on the bed table which she dutifully drank. She lay down, the words of that stage medium still ringing in her head. She could barely remember his name, and yet the way he looked at her, the way he knew... she could not believe that the message was for anyone but her. She could not believe that it was anything but a message from Thomas.

He wanted her to live and love again.

"How, my love?" she asked the darkness. "How do you expect me to go on without you?"

But tonight, she did not cry herself to sleep as she had every night for the past six months. Tonight, she curled on her side and thought of the words given to her. If Thomas was here beside her, she would never wish to trouble him, to make him feel that her sadness was worse than death.

She did not realize that she fell asleep. Instead, she fell into the dream with Thomas's words repeating themselves again and again in her mind.

And then she saw him. She opened her eyes and he was sitting in the chair by the fire, watching her sleep. He looked like he did when they first met, so young and strong. His dark blonde hair was combed neatly, the sides short from where she had trimmed it herself. He was muscle and sinew in the smoldering embers. She could gaze upon him forever, at his high cheekbones and strong nose and perfectly square jaw. She thought every inch of him perfection, even that terrible mustache she always teased that they must shave someday.

"I miss you," she whispered.

He smiled and in that smile was all the love that they had shared together over the years. "Watching your sadness is worse than dying. Do not die while you are still alive, my love. Do not fear to live and love again, Clara."

"I knew that it was you," she said. "I knew you were trying to talk to me earlier."

"Then listen," he replied.

"I do not want to live without you," she confessed.

He crossed to the bed, but it did not move as he sat upon the mattress next to her. "Love again, and soon, my Clara. Have no fear of letting me go."

"It hurts."

"Then let someone help heal your pain. Let someone remind you why living can be a joy. Let someone see that spark of yours that I found irresistible. Love. And know that it is what I want for you..." He reached out, as if to touch her cheek. "Live... and love... for me..."

"I shall try..." she whispered, aching for just one moment more.

But before he could reach her, he disappeared. Instead, she was running, running down that same dark hallway. Only this time, a terrible wind was blowing, was grasping at her and trying to knock her off her feet. She knew there were things in the darkness. She could see their red, glowing eyes. She could make out their terrible shapes. But still she ran.

Suddenly, a feminine voice cut through the terror. "Clara," the girlish voice called. "Clara, I need your help!"

Clara stopped in the maze, listening for the voice to lead her where she needed to go.

"Clara..." came the whisper again.

Clara opened her eyes. The room was bathed in a dim blue light, almost too dim to see. Clara sat up in her bed and asked, "Who said that?"

The form appeared as if Clara was looking at the surface of a glassy lake and something was floating up from the bottom. As it became clearer, the blue glow in the room became stronger until Clara could see everything as if it were bright as day. But as the light grew, the temperature dropped, and Clara found herself shivering and her eyes watering from the cold. Still the form came until Clara could see it was a girl with a face as round and pale as the moon. She was younger than Clara, perhaps fourteen or fifteen years old. She was plump and healthy, dressed in a gauzy purple dress, but her skin was unearthly white. Her strawberry blonde hair was braided and pinned to her head, and she looked at Clara with shy uncertainty.

It was at this moment that Clara realized her eyes were open and they were actually seeing this strange apparition. It wasn't just some dream. She crawled to the edge and looked down. This stranger was floating.

Clara screamed.

She leapt out of bed and ran into the hallway. Almost immediately, she heard pounding steps from the floors below. Mr. Willard and Mrs. Nan raced towards her, Mr. Willard carrying a fireplace poker and Mrs. Nan carrying a light.

"What is it, ma'am?" he asked, ready to face whatever had made Clara scream.

Clara pointed at her room, her heart pounding, unable to form complete sentences. "There is a girl. She is dressed in purple. She is floating. In my room!"

Mr. Willard and Mrs. Nan looked at one another, exchanging a strange glance. Mr. Willard took the lamp, squared his shoulders and walked into the room. Mrs. Nan scooped Clara into her arms to give her comfort, and Clara was grateful for the warmth. Mr. Willard came out, the poker lowered and his stance much more relaxed. "I looked in every corner and checked everywhere, ma'am. I believe your midnight visitor has gone."

Clara looked at Mrs. Nan in confusion and walked into the room. Mr. Willard had spoken the truth. There was no one there. She turned to the two. "But I saw her!"

Mrs. Nan patted Clara's hand and led her to bed. She helped her get her legs under the covers and tucked her in. She brushed back Clara's hair and said, "I know you did. She was just a dream, though. Go to sleep and try to forget all about her. I have a feeling she will not be back tonight."

Clara stared at where the girl had stood. "I know she was here. I saw her. She was right there."

Mrs. Nan and Mr. Willard made for the doorway. "Of course you did," Mrs. Nan reassured. "We'll figure it all out in the morning."

And then the two closed her door.

Clara lay awake, staring at the ceiling. She wasn't one to tell tales, to be frightened by nightmares. She wondered if she was losing her mind, if perhaps it had all been too much and now she was not only condemned to this living, but condemned to hallucinations and flights of fancy.

She rolled over so that she did not have to look at where the girl stood. Try as she might, though, she was unable to fall asleep. The girl's pleas for help rang in her ears as true as when the girl spoke them. Clara kept glancing over to check to see if it was just a trick of the darkness, but the girl did not reappear and everything seemed as it was.

Clara knew better, though.

Chapter Six

Mr. Willard placed the plate before her, a light breakfast of poached eggs and toast. Clara fought to keep her eyes open. The remaining night had been spent wide awake, and she was feeling the effects of it today.

"I apologize for waking you, Mr. Willard," she said.

He gave her a bow and said in his gruff voice, "No need to apologize. A new home oftentimes can create strange dreams. I must confess, I was glad it was nothing more. My ability to chase off ruffians with a poker has, I am afraid, decreased with my age."

Clara picked up her tea cup and took a sip. "We shall have to get you a pistol then."

"And my eyesight is even worse."

Clara imagined Mr. Willard firing blindly in his dressing gown and chuckled.

"It is good to see a smile on your face, ma'am," he said.

She nodded, suddenly aware that the corners of her mouth had turned up for a moment. It was a strange feeling. It was no more than a polite chuckle, but even that was something she had not done for awhile. "I owe you my thanks again, it seems," she replied.

Mr. Willard did not say any more. Instead he changed the subject. "Do you have plans for the day, ma'am?"

She shook her head. "Not really. I will most likely need to have a lie down this afternoon."

"Well, we shall have to have a talk with your dreams and tell them not to wake you this time."

"Mr. Willard?" she asked.

"Yes, ma'am?"

"Have you ever seen a ghost?"

He became very still and lowered his tray upon the sideboard. He did not look at her as he spoke, as if hiding something he did not feel someone should see. "I cannot say, ma'am."

"You have, haven't you...?" she pressed, not letting him disappear into the falsehood he was trying to spin.

"Like I said, my eyesight is not as it once was, and the mind often plays tricks."

"Tell me what you saw, Mr. Willard," Clara asked as she spooned her egg.

He stood stiffly with his hands clasped behind his back. He stared straight ahead. "Once I thought I saw a girl with brown hair, almost a child-like creature, in the hallway. I was hanging a mirror and thought I saw her out of the corner of my eye. I looked in the mirror, though, and saw nothing. I looked again to where I thought she had been standing and she was gone. It was probably only a shadow."

"How strange," said Clara. "Nothing else?"

"No, ma'am. She disappeared and I went about my business."

"Thank you for confiding in me, Mr. Willard."

Her gratitude seemed to put him at ease, this shared moment of secrets opening a door of friendship which perhaps had not been opened before. He smiled at her. "Do not worry about your midnight visitor. I shall look into the matter and make sure that it never happens again."

"How can you swear that I shall never dream of her again, Mr. Willard? You are a most excellent butler, but I do not believe anyone is that good."

"Perhaps it was the dinner which you ate so close to bedtime. A bit too much salt or the wrong combination of dishes. I shall talk to Mrs. Nan about adjusting the menu so that only sweet dreams fill your head."

Clara finished her egg and dabbed her lips with her napkin. "A most excellent suggestion, Mr. Willard. Will you see to it for me?"

"Of course, ma'am."

"You must call me Clara," she said boldly.

"Of course... Mistress Clara, ma'am."

She smiled and rose from the table. "Now, I believe I shall get outside for my stroll before the day gets before me."

"That sounds like a most excellent idea, ma'am."

He made to follow her to the door, but she stopped him. "I shall have Mrs. Nan fetch my things. You have quite enough to do tidying up after my breakfast."

"Very good, ma'am."

She found herself giving him another smile. It seemed rude not to return the goodwill that he bore towards her. She stepped into the foyer and called, "Mrs. Nan! Could you bring me my hat and gloves?"

The housekeeper did not respond, so Clara decided to go upstairs and get them herself.

But as she walked down the hallway, she was struck with a wash of cold. It was as if someone had taken a bucket of ice water and poured it over her head. It reminded her of that cold she felt the night before and instinctively, she looked for the girl in purple. Fear clenched her heart and filled her with foreboding. She could feel its beat pounding in her chest. Her mind screamed at her to fly, to run as far and as fast as she could, but all she could manage was a single step. And suddenly the cold was gone. Her pulse returned to normal. The impending doom melted like sugar in water. She turned back and held out her hand into the space where she just stood and could feel the biting cold of that one spot. Clara walked swiftly to her room to fetch her things and when she came back, edged her way around the area.

Mr. Willard was carrying out the breakfast tray when she reached the ground floor once again.

"Mr. Willard? Have you ever found particularly cold places here in this house?"

He nodded knowingly. "Indeed, ma'am. There are some spots that are quite drafty. It seems as if it is winter in one or two corners. Nothing to worry yourself about, ma'am."

"There was one spot in the middle of the hallway," said Clara, pointing at where she had just been. She thought she saw a look of mild irritation cross Mr. Willard's face, not towards her, but almost towards the location of the cold, the way one might look upon finding a broken shingle on a roof or peeling paint upon a board.

"This house," he muttered. "I shall make sure she moves."

"I am sorry, Mr. Willard. Did you say 'she'?"

The faraway look in his eyes disappeared and he shook his head. "Apologies. I was thinking of your midnight visitor. I meant that I shall make sure we see to the draft."

He stepped down the hallway to take the tray into the kitchen. Clara watched him as he went, wondering if there was perhaps more to her dream than met the eye, and that Mr. Willard meant that 'she' more than he was letting on.

Chapter Seven

Clara settled into her bed, exhausted from so many nights of so little sleep.

The day had passed quietly with no great excitement. She strolled the neighborhood in the morning, pausing to look into shop windows and admire the small garden in front of her house. Curiously, she found herself wandering past the vaudeville house and checking the marquee for the medium. She hated that she had not spoken up during his show and hoped for another chance. Mr. Lowenherz's name was not on the program, though, so she continued on. She returned indoors in the afternoon to explore her new home and rearranged the few things that she brought from her old place. She attempted to nap and failed. And then she sat and waited for the hours to pass.

Dinner was another lovely meal. Chicken glazed with a sweet orange sauce, dessert a small cake with fresh cream. She saw that Mr. Willard meant it quite literally when he said he would ensure her dreams were sweet tonight.

And then the blessed hour of bedtime arrived and once again, she surrendered to the embrace of her pillows. She swaddled herself in her blankets and nestled in. Her eyes closed as the clock struck ten.

"Clara..." whispered a voice.

She was aware of the chimes ringing out midnight. Slowly, sleepily, she lifted her lids. The bedroom was bathed in that same blue light and the girl stood in the corner reaching out to her. The cold returned, causing Clara's teeth to chatter, and perhaps it was more fear than cold that caused her to shake. But this time, she did not scream. Instead, she asked, "What do you want from me?"

The girl waved at her to follow as she passed through the door of the bedroom. There was a part of Clara's mind which wanted to pretend that this was a dream. Or if her mind accepted that it was real, that same part wanted to pretend it was a thief, an intruder of some sort, perhaps a child who lived in the attic and came down to scare her at midnight. But watching the specter pass through the door without opening it would allow her to deny it no longer.

She was seeing a ghost.

Upon the ghost's exit, the room's temperature immediately returned to normal. Clara half hoped she could just stay in bed and pretend that nothing had happened. But then the ghost's hand came through the door, and she curled one delicate, glowing finger and Clara knew she must follow.

Clara wrapped herself in her robe and slid her feet into her slippers. She crept to the door and opened it. The hallway was dark, except for the ghost's unearthly glow at the far end. Clara steeled her courage and stepped forward.

How funny that she would long so much for the afterlife, and here in this moment, she would do anything to escape from it, she thought. She wondered if perhaps her Thomas walked the halls of their old home and felt a pang of regret for leaving. She would do anything in her power to see his face again, living or dead.

She wondered how this young girl had passed, who it was that mourned her loss. Certainly it could not have happened from peaceful means. Though she knew nothing about ghosts besides the stories told in the dark as a child, the fact this one seemed so persistent in her desire to show Clara something, she had to believe there was unfinished business to attend to.

Clara rested her hand upon the wall of her home and was suddenly filled with a sense of such peace. She thought back upon that original sense of kinship with this place and knew that no harm would come to her within its walls.

The ghost continued its journey down the steps and turned into the study. The foyer plunged into darkness as the ghost's light disappeared and Clara was forced to find her way in the pitch black.

She finally stepped into the room and the ghost was pointing at a piece of art upon the wall. It was a hunting painting left by the previous owner. It was hinged on one side and hid the house's wall safe where Clara put her important documents.

The ghost continued to point at it.

"Is it something with the painting?" Clara asked.

The ghost shook her head and pointed again.

"Something in the safe?"

The ghost nodded, a look of relief upon her face.

"I heard you say my name and say that you needed my help. Can you not tell me what it is that you want?"

The ghost's lips moved, but they made no sound. Frustration crossed her face and she became more and more agitated.

Clara held up her hands to calm her. "Please do not fret. I shall open the safe and then you may show me what you need."

But when Clara placed her hand upon the picture, the clock in the hallway struck a quarter past the hour. As the last chime rang, the ghost disappeared.

Clara stood in the darkness in confusion and silence before fumbling her way to a candlestick and lighting it in the banked embers in the fireplace. She did not know what to make of what just happened. She called out, "I do not know if you are still here, but I can no longer see you. I shall look inside the safe and see if I can hazard out your clues. I promise I shall help you rest."

Clara placed the candlestick on a nearby table as she returned to the picture. She swung the frame from the wall and slowly spun the dial of the safe. It took a few attempts, for it was still new and the numbers were not yet familiar. The door finally opened and Clara removed the papers.

They were merely legal documents which would be a shame to lose if someone were to break into her house. Her marriage certificate. Thomas's death certificate. Her accounting records. The deed to the house.

Clara's hand paused upon this document. The home was purchased through a broker and she, herself, had never spoken to the previous owner. She looked at the name -—Lord Horace Oroberg. If strange things were going on, perhaps those who lived here before had experienced it, too.

Clara looked up from the paper. She wondered about the girl who was found dead in this home. She wondered if she was the ghost that Clara saw. Or if the reason she died was because this ghost led her to her doom.

There was only one way to find out. Clara took the deed over to the desk, each step filling her with more certainty. Tomorrow, she would call on Lord Oroberg and she would inquire whether he ever experienced an unwanted houseguest while he lived under this roof.

Chapter Eight

She stood at the front door of the home, her resolve to meet Horace Oroberg swiftly fading. The manor and its grounds were remarkably beautiful. About an hour outside of the city, she had taken the train and then the lovely weather made her decide to walk the country roads to the house. Upon arrival, she wished she had taken a cab so as to appear as if she belonged. A long gravel driveway led to the covered entry, perfect for guests arriving by carriage to step out without worrying about the elements. The gardens were immaculately tended, each hedge perfectly square, each blade of grass in its place. She looked down upon her black dress, now dusty from her travels and hoped she would not receive an immediate dismissal.

She reached to the handle of the doorbell and bravely pulled it. She waited for several minutes, knowing that the house staff most likely had an enormous distance to cross in order to open the door.

Finally, a tall, thin butler peered through the glass. The door swung open and he looked down upon her with such refined distaste, she could barely stop herself from saying she had come to the wrong home and apologize for troubling him.

But she did stand her ground. "Hello. Many apologies for calling without an appointment. I was wondering if Lord Horace Oroberg was available."

The butler sniffed. "And who may I ask is calling?"

She fumbled through her purse and then handed him her calling card. "Mrs. Clara O'Hare. I purchased a home in town from him and had a matter I needed to discuss."

"A matter?"

"Nothing unpleasant, I promise. Just a point of... interest... about the home. I was hoping I might have an opportunity to ask him about its history and something I have come across."

The butler inclined his head slightly. "Please wait and I will see if the master is available."

The door closed and Clara was left standing on the front step. She tried not to show how uncomfortable and out of place she felt. She whispered to herself. "Oh, Thomas. If you were here, you would never have let some butler leave you waiting on a stoop."

Finally, the door opened again. The butler stepped aside and said, "Please come in. Follow me."

The interior of the home was larger than any place Clara had been before. The ceiling extended two stories up. The staircase swooped and the balcony was open, overlooking the foyer. Large potted ferns stood upon marble pedestals. Paintings of ancestors gone by hung from the darkly paneled walls. The butler stopped in front of a double door and opened it.

Clara stepped inside. It was a study, but probably four times the size of the one in her own home. A desk stood at the far end. Several couches were set up around a fireplace. A man rose from his seat upon her entrance. He was an older gentleman, heavyset with the middle aged spread of a man who enjoyed liquor and fine dining. His light brown, graying hair was parted down the middle and swept into two curls on either side of his forehead. His lip sported a walrus-like mustache, which he smoothed before removing his pince-nez from his nose.

The butler announced, "Mrs. Clara O'Hare."

"Thank you, Gilbert. Please have some tea brought in straight away! I'm sure this young lady is quite in need of refreshment." The man stepped forward with his hand outstretched to her. "A pleasure to meet you, Mrs. O'Hare."

"Lord Oroberg?" she asked, trying not to presume.

"At your service." His large hand wrapped around hers like she was but a child. "But please, call me Horace. Jolly good to finally meet you! Lovely to put a name to a person! How is the old place? I hear from my lawyer that you are settled in."

He motioned for her to sit. She lowered herself upon a slipper chair beside the fire as the door opened once again. A tray filled with tea and cookies appeared. The maid poured for both Horace and Clara before disappearing.

"So, tell me. What can I do for you today?" he asked.

Clara picked up the tea, trying to keep the cup from clattering on the saucer. Her hands were trembling and she knew she would look like a fool before this man.

"Tell me, did you ever experience anything strange in that house?" she asked nonchalantly.

"Strange? How?"

She took a sip. Despite knowing that it was of the utmost importance to learn what the ghost was trying to tell her if she ever hoped for an undisturbed night, she began to doubt her reasoning in the bright light of day. "I fear you will take me for a fool."

"What could you ever say that would make me think such a lovely woman as yourself is a fool?" he laughed.

There was a glint in his eye which gave Clara courage. Something which seemed to indicate he might have some personal knowledge of the matter which brought her here.

"I awoke to see a strange figure. A girl. I at first dismissed it as a dream. But the vision returned again last night and whether my imagination or... something else... I was led to believe you might be of aid."

Horace put down his cup and leaned forward, one hand upon his thigh and his face alight in excitement. "You saw her then?"

Clara nodded. "I believe so."

Horace slapped his knee. "I knew it! I knew it. Tell me, what did she look like?"

"A young girl. Red hair. She wore a purple gown."

"That's her all right!" he exclaimed. He sat back and stared at the ceiling. "So many years, and you were the one to see her. I knew that we were not alone in that house."

Clara put down her cup. "I am sorry. Could you please elaborate?"

But he was too excited to hear her words. Instead he got up and began pacing around. "You must be very in tune to be able to actually see her. To see her! Oh, what will the others say? You must come with us this weekend! That is what you must do!"

"I am sorry...?" she questioned, not following his train of thought at all.

"Sorry? There is nothing to be sorry about! You are a sensitive and the answer to our problems! Say you will come!"

"Come where?"

"I will send my soon-to-be daughter-in-law, Violet Nero, to call on you tomorrow and invite you along, just so that you know things are on the up-and-up."

"Please, Lord Oroberg..."

"Horace! You must call me Horace!"

"Horace, please tell me what it is that is going on."

"Why, a séance, of course!"

"A séance?"

"Of course!"

"Why would I want to attend a séance?" Clara asked, a strange thrill coursing through her body.

Horace sat down before her once again. "Because you saw a ghost. An honest to goodness ghost. A ghost who led you here. To me! Don't you want to know why? There are many of us who have had such encounters, people who long for death and yet are not allowed to cross the veil from this living world. Our time may not yet have come, but we feel sympathy with those who have gone before us. They reach out to us almost as much as we reach out to them. I have brought together such friends to explore our experiences. I have hired a medium of excellent repute to come to my home in the north country. So many have said that they have felt and seen things in this particular house of mine. I must know! I must know if it is true!"

"But I saw the ghost in *my* house."

"So, we need to see if it is just that house, or if you are able to see ghosts everywhere. And if you are able to see ghosts any-

where... well... you would have my deepest admiration and re-
gard."

"But I do not know if I want to know if I can see ghosts
everywhere," she protested.

"Of course you do! We are all searching for answers, and
you, my dear, are the closest that any of us have come. The ghost
led you here. On this day of all days! Not a week before or a
week later, but today! Not twenty-four hours since I employed
this medium. It must have been for a reason. This is the only
reason I can think of! You must come spend the weekend with
us. Say that you will!"

Clara sat for a moment in silence. True, she had only come
for answers about the girl in lilac, but Horace's excitement was
contagious. What if she did have some gift? What if this medium could somehow teach her? What if she did not have to wait
until death to see her Thomas again?

It was this final thought which caused her to say, "I will
look forward to meeting your daughter-in-law, Miss Nero, tomorrow, and if we feel a spirit of friendship between us, I shall
indeed look forward to a pleasant weekend in the north country meeting this medium of yours. I thank you kindly for your
invitation and hospitality."

Horace raised his fist in the air in triumph. "Bully! It shall
be a splendid time for all!"

Chapter Nine

Clara sat in her front sitting room. The mid-morning light was pale, but pleasant. Not so dim that it demanded the gas lights be lit, but not so bright that the room became uncomfortably warm. The sound of each passing carriage filled her with both excitement and dread. What would this Violet woman be like? Would they be instant kindred spirits, or would she cause Clara to regret her impetuous decision? Clara played with her wedding band, remembering a time when meeting strangers was a joy. She wondered how it came to be that she became so fearful of her life, how it became so normal to hide indoors. Strangely, it was now her home that became the most unsafe of all, with midnight visitors of the other world variety.

A carriage stopped in front of the house. Clara willed herself not to run to the window to catch a secret glimpse. She heard the front door ring and Mr. Willard's steadfast steps calmly walking down the hall. She heard the door open and murmuring voices. She adjusted her skirts and tucked her hair nervously.

The door to her sitting room opened and Mr. Willard announced the guest. "Miss Violet Nero."

In walked the soon-to-be daughter-in-law of Horace Oroberg. She was a wan creature, almost more bird than human. Her frame was as delicate as a wren. Her large eyes were dark and sunken and her pale skin seemed to almost have a bluish tinge. Her brown hair was pulled back and hung in sausage curls. Though her face held the age of one close to twenty years, she stood no taller than a twelve-year-old girl and her physical development seemed to have ceased at that age, too.

Clara rose. She felt a twinge of instant sympathy for this frail and sickly woman. Who knew what tragedy already struck her. Clara held out both hands in friendship. "Miss Nero. It is a pleasure."

Violet took Clara's hands in hers and allowed Clara to lead her to the seating area. Her voice held the slightest touch of French, as if she held her vowels like candy upon her tongue. "Please, do call me Violet. My father-in-law tells me we have such a great deal in common. I feel that we are to be dear friends."

Violet sat down, perching politely upon the chair, as if frightened to take up too much space. Clara poured milk and sugar into the cups, then filled them both with tea. She passed a saucer to Violet.

"So, you are engaged to Lord Oroberg's son?" Clara asked.

"Indeed. Maman has been friends with the family for a great number of years and says that I am so lucky to have made such a match."

Clara politely sipped, unsure of the way in which Violet spoke of her fiancé through the eyes of her mother's advice.

"But you shall meet Clifford this weekend!" Violet exclaimed, snapping Clara from her thoughts. "Please, do say you will come. It shall be frightfully dull to endure an entire weekend with no one to be my companion besides Maman."

"It sounds like quite a fascinating opportunity," said Clara. "Tell me, who will be joining us?"

"Well, there is Maman and I. Clifford and his father, whom you've already met. Marguerite Matson, who is quite the modern woman. We are not terribly well acquainted, but she has known Clifford since his university days. I hope you will not think poorly of her. When her husband disappeared, she was the center of a great deal of scandal and gossip, but Clifford assures me of her good character. Marguerite is quite the skeptic, though, and has insisted upon bringing a scientist named Norman Scettico to point out the supposed error of our ways. The medium who will be guiding us on our journey is a man named Wesley Lowenherz. He is known in all of the spiritual circles as someone who is quite able to talk to anyone beyond the grave."

At the sound of Wesley's name, she felt the blood drain from her face. She prayed that Violet did not remark at how remarkably pale she had become. Horace had said it was quite a coincidence that she sought him out the moment she did. And how strange a coincidence that of all the mediums in the world, this medium, this Wesley Lowenherz, was the spiritualist he employed. She had been tortured by her cowardice to speak up in that vaudeville house, and now she had been invited to spend an entire weekend in Mr. Lowenherz's presence. Her teacup clattered on its saucer and she placed them both down upon the table. "It sounds like splendid company."

"I am sure it seems quite odd that Horace would be so quick to invite you along, but I promise you shall find our merry party most pleasant."

"It does seem rather strange to go somewhere so far away from town with people I've just become acquainted..." Clara confessed.

Violet nodded, this time seemingly to be the one with the sympathy, which struck Clara as quite a different turn of events. She spoke, "Each of us has endured great tragedy. We have lost loved ones too soon. Each of us wishes to speak with them, to find this connection. Horace is insistent that this home is a place where the veil is quite thin. In fact, Mr. Lowenherz was the first to suggest the location and the company." Violet stared into her cup, almost embarrassed to broach the subject with Clara. "Horace stated that you, yourself, had an experience of a troubling kind."

Clara did not know how best to reply. "At the risk of sounding like quite a madwoman, I saw a strange figure in my chambers the other night and do not know what to make of it."

Violet leaned forward. "And that is why you must come! If you were seeing this figure here, where there is almost no psychic activity at all, imagine who you might see if you join us in this other place! You must come! Please, tell me that you will."

"It could have all been nothing more than a trick of my mind," protested Clara.

"And so you must come to find out if it is just your mind or something more!" Violet whispered conspiringly, "Mr. Lowenherz is the most sought after medium in polite society. His rates are quite beyond your means, or even mine."

Clara did not feel it polite to point out she had seen him just the other day in a line-up at a vaudeville house.

Violet continued, oblivious to Clara's hesitation. "It is only through Horace's intervention that we even have access to him. It is a once in a lifetime opportunity, and you really must come to see if he has answers for you."

Clara was so close to agreeing. There was something about Violet which made Clara immediately trust her. She had such an open vulnerability to her, an innocence that seemed to ask Clara to do the same, and a promise that whatever Clara had seen or endured, it would not be mocked or ridiculed. So, Clara finally dared to ask, "Tell me, have you ever seen anything unworldly before?"

Violet was still for a moment and then nodded. "Yes, when I was a young woman, I thought I saw someone in my room. That vision has stayed with me for all these years and I wonder what he was trying to tell me. I have sought out answers from so many different flim-flam men and frauds. But this Mr. Lowenherz, I have confidence in him. Marguerite has sworn that I am wasting my time and energy again, and this is why she has insisted upon bringing Mr. Scettico, but if there is even a possibility that Mr. Lowenherz can give me answers, well... I cannot think of a better way to spend a few days. And if he is as big a fraud as Marguerite warns, then at least I shall have a lovely weekend in the country with my fiancé and friends." She leaned forward and grasped Clara's hand. "I do hope that you will come, Clara, for I feel as if it was fate which brought us together."

Clara could not cause that hopeful face to fall, and so she found herself replying, "Of course. Of course I will be there as your guest and will look forward to an entertaining weekend of new friendships and adventure."

Violet suddenly seemed alight with joy and excitement. She clapped her hands and declared, "Splendid! I shall send a carriage round for you Friday afternoon!"

Her enthusiasm was infectious, and Clara found herself strangely looking forward to this surprise holiday. She felt as if saying yes to this kind invitation was a step forward. If her isolation was causing her late husband sadness beyond the grave, she would try to live. She would try her best to bring him joy once again.

Chapter Ten

The carriage rocked gently along the muddy path. A low mist hung over the boggy fields and the sky was darkening threateningly. Horace Oroberg's house in the north country was two hours by rail and then another hour by carriage ride. Despite the luxury in which Clara traveled, she was exhausted and looked forward to arriving at her final destination.

The horse's hooves clomped across a long bridge over a steep bank. Clara looked down and saw that the river below was already high. The storm clouds must have broken upstream already and caused the rain to gather. From the speed of the water, she could see that the storm would be violent.

Far ahead, she could see the country house. The lights shone warmly from the windows. She wondered how she would appear arriving in such a splendid place, her in her mourning clothes as all the others gathered to reach out to dead ones. She thought of the assumptions that others would make about her, so sure that it was her husband she wished to reach. She wondered, as she stared at the house, why she had not sought him out in the spiritual realm before. Perhaps it was her own skepticism of such things, of charlatans who preyed upon the weak and grieving. And yet, here she was. If it had not been for her own strange experience in her little house upon the square, she never would have ventured into such passings. She hoped that this was not some ill-fated ruse. She could not think of any reason someone might go to such effort and expense to swindle her. Indeed, her new home and her pension were the only wealth she had, and while comfortable for a woman living alone, they were not sizeable enough to be attractive to a con artist. She knew her only defense would be to keep her wits about her and to keep herself from falling under the spell of proceedings.

The carriage pulled up to the house and as the driver removed her baggage, Horace's butler, Gilbert, emerged to lend his hand as she climbed out and gather her things.

"Good to see you again, Gilbert," she said.

"Ma'am," was all he replied.

She walked into the home. Immediately, she was struck by the sheer masculinity of the decor. She had not thought that there might not be a Mrs. Oroberg, but now it dawned on her that perhaps Horace's overtures of friendship might possibly tend towards a friendship she was not entirely comfortable with. Had he invited her here as a guest of his daughter-in-law to have an opportunity outside the bounds of societal propriety? She hoped that she was jumping to wild conclusions.

Gilbert led her through the front hall filled with hunting trophies. There were heads of antelope, zebras, and buffalo hanging over every door. He ushered her into the library where tusks of ivory framed the fireplace and Zulu spears adorned the walls. Skins of tigers and leopards were scattered upon the furniture like blankets. The foot of an elephant served as the base for a table. A great bear rug spread out before the fire. Clara thought it no wonder that Horace believed this home seemed so connected with death. There was death at every turn.

The door opened and a man entered. He was a rakish figure. His curling brown hair was carelessly styled in such a way that she could tell his valet fussed over it for hours. He wore his dinner coat and tie with the ease of a man used to finery. There was a lazy look to his eyes, a curl to his lips of insolent knowing, a swagger to his stance that showed he was a man not used to hearing the word "no". He carried a glass of scotch and threw it back the moment he looked at her, his eyes never leaving her face. He strode across the room. "Mrs. O'Hare! My father has told me so much about you!"

He took her hand in his and raised it, his lips lingering on her fingers far longer than politeness would allow.

"I believe I have had the pleasure of meeting your fiancée," she replied, removing her hand from his.

He took his empty glass and decided the best place for it would be the mantle directly behind her. But rather than comfortably walk around, he leaned into her, so close that his body almost touched hers. "Pardon me," he murmured, his mouth dangerously close.

"Oh, leave the poor widow alone," came a voice from across the room.

Clara looked up to see who this savior was. It was a woman about her age. She wore a tightly bodiced gown of blood red, which held her figure in a perfect hourglass. The high-necked daywear had been exchanged for the scooped neckline of the night. It fell from her shoulders revealing her elegant carriage and enticing bosom. Her black hair was large and loose, pinned up in the Gibson style that Clara had seen on the front cover

of a *Life Magazine* only a few weeks before. Her high chiseled
cheek bones framed her shocking blue eyes, eyes that looked
upon the world with bored detachment.

"Whatever Marguerite wishes, she gets. Those are the rules,
aren't they?" Clifford asked as he backed away from Clara with
knowing humor, as if delighting in how uncomfortable he
made her for that moment. He leaned over and planted a kiss
upon Marguerite's cheek. The woman appeared utterly unin-
terested in his affections.

"You have a fiancée now, Clifford, and you will need to behave yourself if you hope to weasel your way into her dead dad-
dy's dowry."

"Such dreadful accusations from you, Marguerite! How
dare you insinuate such awfulness!" he replied in mock horror.

She took a sip from her wide champagne glass and peered
at him over the rim. "Am I wrong?"

"I should have married you."

"Your money is not green enough for my taste," she replied.
She held out an outstretched hand to Clara and daintily
gripped her fingers. "You mustn't pay us the slightest bit of
attention. Clifford and I have been school chums since he
learned how to look up a girl's skirt. He's all bark and, pitifully,
no bite."

"A pleasure to make your acquaintance," said Clara, feeling
adrift in this sea of inside jokes and politics.

Marguerite looked upon her, taking in her attire in such
a way that Clara felt she should apologize for not making the
mark. "Black. I suppose you are in mourning for someone near
and dear, so near and dear you would allow yourself to be led
into this lion's den of poor manners and bad taste."

"I confess, I do not know entirely what I am getting myself into. I was invited here by Violet..."

Marguerite rolled her eyes and flung her curved body upon a chair. "Oh, shy little Violet. So anxious for a friend to share in her hare-brained adventures. My condolences."

"Really, she seemed quite kind..." said Clara.

"The fact you are here is a mark against her 'kindness'," stated Marguerite.

"Now, don't go scaring off such pleasant company," said Clifford. He touched Clara's chin and tilted her head towards the fire to get a better look at her features. "Fine company and fine to look at, too."

"Clifford, you had better find yourself on the other side of the room before Violet and that mother of hers get here."

He sighed. "They are all the way on the other end of the house preparing the room with the medium."

"Oh, that's why I came in. They are done and on their way."

Clifford ran over to the other side of the library and planted himself at the farthest window.

"Coward," Marguerite laughed, downing her drink.

At that moment, the sound of voices filled the hallway. Clara was unsure whether to sit or stand, to go towards the door or remain where she was. The entire evening had her flustered and everything was sixes and sevens.

The door opened and in came Horace, with Violet's delicate hand upon his massive forearm. Behind them came a woman that Clara could only suppose was Violet's mother. She had darker hair than her daughter, but shared the same large, permanently-startled eyes. Her hair was gathered upon her head in a loosely held bun. Her wasp-like waist was cinched into an hourglass, which took some doing for this woman was almost skeletal with skin hanging loosely from her bones. Her face was pinched, as if the smell of sour milk lurked beneath her nose. She was escorted by a man with mutton chop sideburns and a humorless, shrew-like face.

But it was not this couple who captured Clara's attention. No, it was the man who followed them behind. As he entered, it felt as if all the air had been taken from the room. She had seen him once before, upon the stage in that vaudeville house, but that did not prepare her for what it was like standing next to him in the flesh. Clara felt the blood rush to her face and chest as a strange heat washed through her body.

This unwanted, visceral response seemed a betrayal of Thomas. And yet, she could not stop it. A warmth, a silence, a moment of stillness seemed to descend upon the room as Wesley Lowenherz became the only thing she could see. She tried to push this sensation away, but she had no more power than a person who tries to stop the room from spinning after too many glasses of champagne.

It had been like this with her Thomas.

One look, and he had claimed her heart.

And now, this Wesley Lowenherz.

Watching your sadness is worse than dying. Do not die while you are still alive, my love. Do not fear to live and love again. The words rang in her memory, spoken in a dream by the love of her life, but also from the very real lips of this very real man who stood before her. Something about him claimed a part of her she did not think she was ready to give away again.

But off the stage and out of the greasepaint, he was more dashing than she ever thought possible. If anything, the stage had made him seem smaller and less than his own reality. He was still tall and slim with broad shoulders, square jawed and heavy browed. He still had that beautiful head of wavy, auburn hair that caught the light so magically. But his skin was so clear, she could tell he did not partake of a single drop of liquor. There was a rarified power in his movement and a gentlemanly way in which he carried himself. A soulfulness to his brown, dark eyes. They were soft and warm, as if incapable of an angry glance. They fixed upon Clara and she was unable to break from their gaze.

Wesley stepped closer and she could feel her pulse pounding in her ears. Clara was aware of someone talking, of introducing people to her, but it wasn't until Horace said, "And may I introduce Mr. Wesley Lowenherz?" that she heard anything.

Wesley reached for her hand, which she gave gladly. His touch was electric, and the sensation of his lips upon the back of her hand was as intimate as if he had brushed across her mouth instead.

"My deepest condolences for your loss," he said.

Those words brought Clara back into the room and broke the spell. She was aware once more of her clothes of mourning, of the figure of a grieving widow she cut, and of how, until this very moment, she expected to spend the rest of her life as such. But the human heart has its own plans and, inexplicably and unwarranted, his spirit and manner seemed to be a pinprick of light which cracked her world of darkness. She nodded, choking down the urge to correct him, to tell him that for the first time in a long time, things might not always be as they seemed.

Instead, she merely said, "A pleasure to make your acquaintance."

Horace introduced her to the others. Hilda Nero, Violet's mother, and Norman Scettico, the scientist that Violet had spoken to her about. But Clara barely paid attention. Instead, she was entranced by this Mr. Lowenherz, following him with her eyes as he sat down next to Marguerite, as he spoke with Violet, as he greeted Clifford. *What is going on?* Clara wondered as she fought with herself and lost. *Why am I behaving like a besotted schoolgirl?*

She could almost imagine Thomas laughing at her.

The conversation was interrupted by the ringing of the dinner gong.

Horace rose to his feet and said, "If you all would follow me into the dining room, I believe dinner is now served."

Gilbert opened the double doors between the sitting room and the dining room. An elegant table was laid with service for five courses. Horace took the head of the table with his son taking the other end. Clara felt the color rise to her cheeks as she realized she was seated across from Mr. Lowenherz.

After the drinks were poured, Horace lifted his glass and declared, "To the life beyond!"

They all lifted their glasses in agreement. Or almost all.

Norman Scettico placed his glass back onto the table without joining in the toast. "I hope that we shall all keep an open mind so that we might discern between the truths and fictions that we see tonight."

Horace gave him a laugh. "I am sure that your cunning eye will pierce through any charlatan's trick, but since we have here as our guest one of the greatest mediums society has ever known, I am sure that you can sit back to enjoy the evening, safe in the knowledge that there is nothing more to discern, for the truth has already revealed itself."

The table politely tittered, but Norman gave a cold glare as he bit his tongue and kept from answering back. His sip from his wine glass was large.

As the soup was brought out and served, Mr. Lowenherz turned to Clara, casually enquiring, "I am acquainted with the history of our other guests, Mrs. O'Hare, but do not know what brings you to our circle tonight."

She placed down her spoon, feeling the eyes of the entire table upon her. She felt her mouth go dry and prayed that she not seem a fool before them. "I had a midnight visitor the other day who led me to Horace... I believe she is one of the other world. Upon calling on Horace, it seemed natural that I should join your merry group this weekend to see if perhaps some answers might be gleaned as to who she is and why she is in such distress."

Mr. Lowenherz looked at Clara with even greater interest, which she found she did not object to in the least. "Truly? I would have guessed from your attire you would have wished to be reunited with a loved one recently passed."

Clara swallowed, strangely not wanting to dissuade his attentions, but knowing she must acknowledge his observation. "I am sure that we all might wish to speak again to those who have gone before us, but that is not what brought me here tonight."

"May I ask who it was who left?"

"You are the medium. Perhaps you should tell me," Clara laughed, but not sure anymore if she wanted to hear Thomas's words spoken by this man.

"Do you believe in an afterlife, Mrs. O'Hare?" he asked.

She found herself unable to answer at first, fearful that she might lose her composure. Finally she managed to say, "I hope there is. I hope that we shall all be reunited with those we hold dear. This other figure that appeared to me seemed to make me think that there is life beyond. But I no longer feel as though I understand what it looks like or what it means. Perhaps it is the answers to that very question which causes me to come here today."

Mr. Lowenherz smiled at her warmly, as if to encourage her to have faith. But then the sharp voice of Mr. Scettico cut into their discussion. "Whether there is or is not makes no difference. The question is whether man is capable of speaking to those who have passed. I have yet to see someone who is actually capable of such a feat."

"Perhaps you shall be surprised tonight," said Mr. Lowenherz. "There is, after all, a first time for everything."

"I find the fleecing of mourning widows and children to be the lowest form of humanity, Mr. Lowenherz," he replied.

"Then you and I are of one mind," said the medium.

Norman opened and shut his mouth with irritated annoyance, bothered that Wesley did not seem to understand that *he* was the villain Norman was so violently against. To point it out would border upon outright rudeness, and Clara got the sense that Norman was not the sort of man to take such an outward stand. So, instead, he glowered into his soup, as if willing that the bits and pieces within would cause Mr. Lowenherz's eyes to be opened to the fraud that he most assuredly was.

Clara, on the other hand, felt hope for the first time. She felt as if this man, this Wesley Lowenherz, might hold the answers. She wondered what it might take to have him come to her home. She thought of that for a moment, cutting quite the heroic figure as he called up the spirits and vanquished them from her house. She thought of how grateful she would be and how, perhaps, he might allow her to express that gratitude. She took another sip of wine, sure that it was the drink and exhaustion which caused her senses to stray.

"Well," said Mr. Lowenherz finally, breaking the awkwardness of Norman's outburst. "After dinner, we shall see the test of my talents and hopefully you shall all be reassured that this evening was not a waste."

Horace slapped the table. "What is taking these courses so long? I say we skip straight to the pudding and get it over with."

The sharp, shrill voice of Violet's mother, Hilda, cut through his enthusiasm with her mannered rule. "Of all the ridiculous ideas. To force one's guests to speed through their evening meal all for the sake of meeting up with spirits that have nowhere better to be. They shall be hanging about for all eternity. I should suppose they would be quite grateful to have someone to talk to every now and again. Speed through to the pudding, indeed."

Horace immediately calmed himself, patting his lip with his napkin. "Of course, Hilda. My enthusiasm got the better of me."

"Just look at poor Violet! Withering like a flower in the sun with barely enough sustenance to keep her going. All of this because you want to talk to some ghosts? We are lucky this Mr. Scettico is here to point out the folly of your ways, Horace."

"Now, Hilda, you were once just as entranced as I am with these matters. Just because you were taken for a fool once does not mean that all mediums are scam artists, out to part you from your fortune."

"I am sure I provide myself as quite a target. Grieving for the loss of a son and then to have someone come along and take advantage."

"I am sure that Mr. Lowenherz is above such dastardly deeds. He is well aware any trickery on his part will cause us to prosecute him with every ounce of the law, aren't you Mr. Lowenherz?"

Wesley practically choked on his dinner. He looked up, eyes watery from coughing. "Quite," he assured.

Violet picked at her food, but was not eating any of it. "It would be lovely to speak to Victor once more."

"Was that your brother?" asked Clara politely.

"Indeed," said Violet. "He passed when I was quite young."

"Maybe he can tell you where that father of his hid your inheritance," jested Clifford. His face was beet red from the wine and it was plain to see that he was not in a good frame of mind to be making such jokes.

But Marguerite leaned forward, with interest. "Really? I was unaware that it disappeared."

"This is not polite dinner conversation," muttered Hilda, sawing her knife through her mutton.

"Quite impolite, Marguerite," Clifford slurred. "Although, wouldn't it be funny if we learned your husband and Violet's papa were shacked up at the seaside this whole time, living off of all that wonderful Nero money?"

"You're drunk, Clifford," Marguerite stated. She did not even attempt to hide her contempt. Violet stirred the food upon her plate and pretended that he had not said anything so uncouth.

"And what of you?" Clara asked Horace, trying to shift the focus of the conversation delicately. "Who do you seek out?"

Horace waved her question away. "Oh, a little of this. A little of that. It is the last great frontier, isn't it?" He pointed at all of the animals stuffed and hung in the room, from the polar bear on one side to the ostrich on the other. "I have visited every corner of the globe. I have faced the fiercest animals known to man. And yet, here is one beast I cannot tame. One beast that I cannot slay. I might be able to choose between life or death for each of these creatures, but there is the great hunter in the sky who stalks me and one day will take me down with a blow to my heart or a crack to my skull or perhaps a fit of pneumonia or an infected hangnail. One way or another, death will come. What I have learned from hunting, though, is that you must know your enemy if you want to avoid him. You must know his methods and his habits if you want to stay one step ahead. That's what I hope to find by piercing the veil. Answers! Answers to this life, to this mystery, to death! I want to know the things that will help me sidestep the Reaper until the days become too much of a burden and I look forward to sitting down with him over a bourbon. That's what I hope."

They all quietly mulled over his words. Then Norman spoke up. "You do realize there is no 'Reaper'..."

Horace became red in the face and started to sputter. "Who invited this joy killer to our weekend anyways?" He shook his finger in Norman's direction. "You'll best keep your opinions to yourself. If I say there is a Reaper and he is haunting me, then I'll be damned if some know-nothing who has never stared down the barrel of danger and laughed in its face will tell me he knows what's what. You keep your opinions to yourself, sir, and I shall make sure to give you a wide berth."

They spent the rest of the evening eating in awkward silence. Any attempt at polite conversation fell lamely to the side and the speaker felt that perhaps they were better off not having said anything at all.

Finally, the last course was served—an excellent dessert of blood oranges and brandy—and Horace pushed himself back from the table. "Now, if we have all eaten and drunk our fill, or at least eaten and drunk to the satisfaction of Hilda here, since she is now our resident expert on other people's stomachs, we can retire to the other room and let the festivities begin."

They all stood and began walking towards the parlor.

As Gilbert began to clear their places, Horace turned back and blustered. "Gilbert! Tell the house staff to get home to their cottages. They can clean up this mess in the morning."

"Sir?" he asked.

"You heard me right. You stay in case we need anything, but I'll not have this one," he pointed at Norman, "saying that the noises we hear were them banging around, or worse that they were in cahoots with Mr. Lowenherz here. And I, personally, don't want them wandering in and interrupting our proceedings. You tell them all to get out now."

"But the storm, sir," said Gilbert, pointing at the rain which was starting to fall.

"Well, tell them to leave immediately so that they don't get caught in this mess. Hurry up now! And I don't want to hear another sound from you until we leave the séance room, do you understand?"

Gilbert bowed low. "As you wish, sir."

Chapter Eleven

They went into the parlor. The heavy, velvet curtains had been drawn so that not even the moonlight could enter. Though there were gas lamps upon the walls, they were turned off and the room was only lit with flickering candles dripping from brass candelabras. The room had dark flooring and dark furniture and a dark organ that appeared to never have been played. The face of a wild boar sprang out of the shadows and Clara stifled her instinct to scream. It was only a trophy from one of Horace's conquests. But just as she was about to think how she wished that Thomas was here to reassure her, Wesley kindly placed his hand upon her elbow. She looked up at him in surprise. His gentle eyes met hers, and he seemed to say, without words, that he would let no harm come to her, that there was nothing to fear. She thought how strange it was that he knew, somehow, that she needed this simple gesture.

In the middle sat a round table with a red velvet cloth draped over it. Eight seats circled it, waiting for the guests.

The eeriness of the room seemed not to affect Horace. He strode in and plopped himself upon a chair. "So, is this where I sit, eh Wesley?"

Clara and Marguerite exchanged glances over this broach in protocol—Clara with embarrassment, Marguerite with amusement. Mr. Lowenherz cleared his throat, but did not correct the man.

"Indeed, Lord Oroberg. In fact," Wesley motioned to the entire company, "Please, find the place at the table which makes you feel the most comfortable. There are resonances in the spirit world which will become in tune with your harmonics. Your energy will create a chord of harmony to invite your loved ones through."

Norman sniffed. "In that case, might I request a chair in the hall?"

Clifford drunkenly slapped him on the back. "Now, now, sir. Are you in league with this man? Wanting a chair outside to pull the table strings and ring the tambourine? You almost had us fooled by your misanthropic ways, but I am on to you now, sir." Clifford sat down, his legs spread wide and patted the two seats beside him. "I believe the spirits are telling me that I should have Marguerite and Mrs. O'Hare within easy reach."

Clara looked at poor Violet. The only betrayal of her feelings was a small hiccup of breath. Clara took the girl by the shoulders and gently guided her over to her fiancé. "I am quite sure that the spirits would be much happier to have you seated beside your bride-to-be."

Violet gave her a tight but grateful smile. Hilda's mother sat on the other side of her, as if daring Clifford to behave badly in her presence, and Marguerite sat Norman next to the man, using her scientific friend as a buffer between her and Clifford's unscientific approaches. Unintended, Clara found that the only seat which remained was beside Wesley's empty chair. She sat down and wondered how the rapid beating of her heart might affect the appearance of spirits.

As soon as everyone was seated, Wesley walked around the room, extinguishing the candles so that only one candelabrum remained. He picked it up and brought it over, placing it in the center of the table. He sat down. "Now, if we could all take hands."

He took Clara's hand in his. His hand was soft and warm, and she wanted to believe that as he adjusted his fingers, it was not just comfort that caused him to caress his thumb gently against her skin.

"Take hands? This is the oldest trick in the book. You'll move the table with your feet and start dancing on a tambourine with your toes," said Norman in a superior tone.

Wesley shifted uncomfortably, most likely to keep from saying something he would later regret. Instead, he pointed out: "I allowed each of you to pick your seat. If I had trickery in mind, I would have reserved my seat where my wires and mirrors were close at hand. Now, if we can begin..."

Norman harrumphed.

"Please, sir. The spirit world will not make itself known to us if it senses it is not welcome," Wesley said.

"Shut your trap, Norman," bellowed Horace. "I didn't drag all of us out to the middle of nowhere to hear you yammer on. Let's get on with it! Bring on the ghosts!"

Once more, Wesley seemed to stifle the words he clearly wanted to say. Clara gave his hand a gentle squeeze of encouragement. He looked over at her in gratitude and his smile was enough to cause her to look down in pleased embarrassment.

"If you all would close your eyes..." Wesley began.

"I'm not closing my eyes!" spat Norman.

"You'll close your eyes or you'll find yourself walking to the train station in this rain!" shouted Horace.

Wesley began again. "If you would all close your eyes and breathe deeply. Think of the person you wish to contact and gently invite them to join our circle."

Clara watched as each person closed their eyes, occasionally reopening them to check and see if everyone else was participating. She shut her eyes and in the darkness thought of the girl who had appeared to her. She wanted to think of Thomas, to invite his presence, but for some reason, could not bring herself yet to face him, not when she found her hand clasped in Wesley's warmth, and not wanting to pull away.

"Now, if you would all open your eyes," said Wesley. He then called out. "We ask those spirits in the room to make themselves known."

A tinkling bell rang from a far corner and a chill ran down Clara's back.

"I don't know if we should be doing this," Clara whispered, the fear building within her.

The sound of the bell was matched with the sound of a tambourine.

"It is Peter!" shouted Hilda for some reason. "Peter has come back! Where did you leave the money, Peter?"

The table shifted beneath them and all but Wesley, who sat with his head still bowed and eyes closed, shouted in alarm.

That was when Clara looked behind his left shoulder. "I see her!" she shouted. "I see her there!"

Wesley's eyes opened and he stared at Clara. "What do you see?"

"Behind you! The girl who came to me!"

Wesley looked behind him, as did everyone else.

"Do you not see her?" Clara asked, begging for someone to confirm that this was not a hallucination, but she seemed alone in this vision.

"Tell us what she looks like," commanded Wesley.

Clara looked at the girl, who was staring blankly at Clara. "She is young, younger than me. Perhaps fourteen or so. She has light, red hair braided and pinned to her head. She wears a dress of lilac. Her face is round and her skin freckled."

Wesley's face looked as if he had just endured a slap. "Ask her if her name is Minnie."

"Are you Minnie?" Clara repeated.

The girl immediate looked up, staring deep into her eyes and nodded.

"Yes! Yes, she is Minnie!" Clara confirmed.

At that moment, lightning flashed and a roll of thunder boomed so loudly it caused the entire room to shake. Minnie looked around her in fear. She seemed to be trying to say something.

"Minnie! Minnie, what is it?" Clara shouted.

The window flew open and the rain poured into the room. The wind from the storm blew out the candle and they were plunged into darkness.

"Be not afraid!" Wesley commanded.

"Gilbert!" Horace yelled. "Gilbert! Bring us a light!"

The door to the room was flung open by the butler and the light from the hallway shone in.

They all sat, hands still clasped and the terror of the moment passed.

And then they realized that Hilda sat there in their circle, dead, with her neck snapped and lolling unnaturally to the side.

Chapter Twelve

Violet screamed at the sight of her mother. She buried her face in Clifford's chest, who awkwardly tried to provide some comfort. His face was so pale, he himself might have been mistaken for a ghost. Wesley was immediately upon his feet, lighting the candles to chase away the darkness. Norman ran to the poor woman, his fingers upon her throat, searching for a pulse.

"She's dead," he confirmed.

"Of course she is dead!" shouted Clifford. "Her head has practically been snapped from her body." Violet gave a muffled cry. Clifford patted her shoulder bracingly. "Apologies, dear. But it is."

Marguerite was on her feet at once, searching the floor as if for footprints or some sort of clue. "How in the devil did someone get in here to do this?"

They all stared, the open window continuing to flap open and shut in the wind, but no longer with the violence of its initial swing.

"Who said someone had to get in to do it?" said Norman accusingly.

Marguerite rolled her eyes, "We were all holding hands. We would have known if someone let go." She looked at each person individually. "Did anyone let go?" They all shook their heads and she turned back to Norman. "Then that means someone got in and did it."

Wesley walked over and closed the window, latching it tight.

Horace pointed his finger accusingly at Wesley. "I said we wanted to see ghosts, not be ghosts!"

Norman joined in his reproach. "You're the flim-flam man here. You tell us how this happened!"

The color drained from Wesley's face. "My dear sir, if you are insinuating I had anything to do with this death..."

"You're in cahoots with that widow!" Norman replied, now pointing at Clara. "You and your false stories of fake ghosts dressed in purple. You distracted us while the murderer got in!"

"What?" Clara said, aghast.

"None of us have ever seen you before tonight. And despite the fact all of us have occupied a room together in the past, none of us have ever ended up dead until you showed up."

Clara gulped. "Do you mean to say that I killed this woman?"

"I can assure you that her hand never left mine," Wesley said, stepping forward to protect her if Norman continued his rant.

Horace waved away Norman's accusations. "Please. A woman's delicate touch could not have done such an act. Strangulation, perhaps, but snapping another woman's neck? She wouldn't have the strength. And you call yourself a scientist! I find your powers of observation do not fill me with confidence in your skills."

Norman pulled down the bottom edge of his waistcoat, as if Horace was throwing down a challenge. "Fine. So, it needs to have been a man with strong hands who was not in our circle. Is that what you're saying?"

The entire room stopped. As one, they all turned and looked at Gilbert, hulking Gilbert, with his massive hands and long arms.

"I swear to you all that it was not me," the butler protested.

Horace stepped forward speaking slowly so that there could be no misunderstanding. "Gilbert, did you send home all of the house staff as I requested?"

Gilbert's eyes were wide, aware of how bad this appeared. "I did, sir. We are quite alone."

"It was him! It was him, I say!" shouted Norman. "The butler did it!"

Horace waved him down and turned back to Gilbert. "You realize that I am forced to confine you to your rooms, Gilbert, until the police are able to conduct a full investigation."

The butler nodded but did not make any protest. "I understand fully, sir, the unfortunate situation as it appears to be."

"Very well. If someone would care to come with me to witness the confinement. I won't have it be said that I let a faithful servant escape because of old loyalties or some such rot."

"I would be happy to go with you," offered Wesley quietly, trying to let Gilbert know he would not condemn him until his guilt was proved.

"Not you! I do not trust you as far as I can throw you!" said Norman.

"Fine, Norman! You come along then, too!" snapped Horace.

"Why do you all act as if I am committing some great wrong by pointing out the truth of what is going on?" asked Norman.

"I was the fool who brought you here. I will be the fool to put up with your nonsense," said Marguerite as she took Norman's elbow. She gave Horace a little wave. "Norman and I will go with you." She then turned back to the remaining group. "Wesley? Stay here and make sure that Clifford doesn't do anything untoward towards the girls, will you?" Clifford opened and closed his mouth like a fish in protest. "Don't pretend, Clifford. It is unseemly. Lead the way, Horace!"

Horace nodded gruffly and motioned for Gilbert to walk in front of him. They all marched out of the room, leaving Wesley, Clifford, Violet, and Clara to keep poor Hilda's body company.

Violet was sobbing quietly into Clifford's shoulder. He kept looking over at her mother's body uncomfortably. "There, there. No one liked her very much in the first place."

Violet gave a violent gasp and pushed him away.

Clara rushed over to embrace her as Clifford realized his callousness. With her arm around Violet's shoulders, Clara tactfully suggested, "Perhaps you would like to see Violet to her room, where she can lie down until the police arrive."

Clifford seemed immediately relieved to have some sort of helpful direction in this moment of crisis. He gently guided Violet to her feet and towards the door, looking highly uncomfortable by her emotional outbursts.

"Quite the happy couple, aren't they?" Wesley remarked under his breath.

Clara looked over at him. "Your thoughts mirror my own."

He grimly smiled, as if he was unaware that he had spoken those words aloud. "Apologies. It was an inappropriate comment in such a moment of tragedy."

Clara shook her head. "I find it the most appropriate of sentiments. Her own mother, killed before her, and him unable to manage. Poor thing. She deserves better than that."

Wesley stared at the dead woman. "And so we find ourselves in the uncomfortable position, Mrs. O'Hare, of deciding what to do next."

"Please, call me Clara. I find that enduring a murder is an occasion to drop formalities."

He reached over and gripped her hand and she gripped his hand back. She could not help but to think how grateful she was to have him here to offer his strength if she needed it. She tried not to imagine what this night would have been like without him. It would have been beyond endurance.

And then she realized she had been standing there for some minutes, just holding on to him, without saying a word. She cleared her throat. "Perhaps we should contact the authorities."

Wesley held her hand for a moment longer before giving it a squeeze and heading out of the room. "Of course. That is a most sensible course of action."

There was a phone hung in the hallway. Clara had never used one before, but Wesley made straight for it. She followed behind. He picked up the black receiver and placed it to his ear. He jiggled the hook. "Hello?" He spoke into the mouthpiece on the wall. "Hello?" Disappointed, he placed the receiver back in its crook. "The line appears to be dead."

Clara looked out towards the windows. "Most likely this storm has severed the lines. We shall have to ride into town."

Wesley nodded grimly and strode towards the front door. He opened it up and was greeted by sheets of rain. Clara peered out from around his steady frame.

"You cannot take a carriage," she said. "The wheels would get stuck in the mud within a few minutes of being on the road."

"I shall go by horseback, then," he replied.

She cautioned, "Perhaps it is best to wait until morning."

He turned, placing both hands upon her arms in a gesture which was strangely protective and familiar for one she had just met. "There is a murderer in the house and a dead woman in the parlor. As much as I would enjoy spending the evening here with you before a warm fire, there is no time to wait."

She nodded in understanding, respecting him even more for placing himself in harm's way in order to ensure their safety... her safety... She reached over to the stand and took a hat and overcoat from the hook. She passed them to him. "Be safe, then."

He took the hat from her and placed it upon his head, and allowed her to hold the jacket as he fit his arms into the sleeves. Out of habit and without thinking, she found herself smoothing the shoulders and turning him to straighten the front lapels like she used to do for Thomas. She stopped herself, realizing her hands now rested upon the strong muscles of his chest and she was standing too close for a woman who was not his wife. He looked upon her, his brown eyes smoldering with something more than just duty as they gazed at one another.

"Promise me you will be safe, Clara. I would be most distressed if something were to happen to you while I was away."

She smiled, picking a bit of lint from his collar, the gesture strangely intimate. "I shall promise you that gladly."

He nodded once more and then stepped away to stride into the darkness. Clara watched him for as long as she could see him, which was not all of ten steps. The rain was fierce and blowing almost sideways. Lightning lit up the sky and for another moment, she saw his silhouette against the sky. She hoped that she would see him again.

Chapter Thirteen

S he closed the door. The sound of feet came from the hallway behind her and she turned. Horace, Marguerite, and Norman emerged.

"All is well?" she asked.

"As well as it could be," said Horace. "Damnable surprise this. Who would have thought Gilbert, after all these years of service, would sink to such violence? No accounting for the help these days. You treat them fairly. You give them a home and shelter and honest work, and they then go kill a woman in your own parlor. Well, I shall think twice before hiring a butler stronger than myself, I tell you!"

Marguerite rolled her eyes. "Please, Horace. Let the police determine his guilt before you play judge and jury."

Horace didn't make a reply, just harrumphed and looked towards the parlor uncomfortably. "Well, I suppose we should decide what to do with Hilda next."

"You should leave the crime scene untouched so that the police can do their jobs!" Norman insisted in his whiny pitch.

"Be quiet, Norman," Marguerite sighed.

"Wesley... I mean... Mr. Lowenherz has left to fetch the authorities," said Clara.

"Went out in this storm?" Horace pointed at the phone. "He could have called!"

Clara shook her head. "Wesley tried, but I'm afraid he said the lines are down."

"Does he even know how a telephone works?"

"He seemed familiar enough with it. I'm sure he was doing it correctly." Clara pointed outside, "The rain and wind really is so terrible, a tree must have interfered."

"Well, a damnable nuisance that." Horace peered out the window. "He went into that storm, then? I hope we don't have two bodies to deal with come morning."

"Horace, please," Marguerite said. "Things are getting downright morbid."

"There is a dead woman in the parlor, Marguerite," Norman pointed out.

"That is still no reason to go losing our heads."

"Like her?"

Marguerite gave him a look which caused him to shut up. "We are going to go into the dining room and are going to help ourselves to a drink to steady our nerves. And then we are going to wait until the police arrive and get this whole mess sorted. And then we were going to go to bed and wake up in the morning and deal with whatever the day deals us. Do you all understand?" she asked. Her tone brooked no nonsense and the entire company seemed quite happy to allow her to take command of the situation.

"Thank you," Clara murmured to Marguerite as they entered the dining room.

"For what? For finding an excuse to empty Horace's liquor cabinet without looking like a callous drunk? We should be thanking Hilda. He'll break out the good stuff, now."

Clara stood still for a moment, and Marguerite did not seem to notice that she did not keep pace.

Really, thought Clara, what a houseful of horrible human beings she found herself trapped with. She looked back at the door, wondering if Wesley was still safe or lost in the rain and when he might return. She wondered for a moment if she should perhaps go out and search for him so that he was not traveling alone when Marguerite placed a tumbler full of something in her hands.

"Cheers! Hilda is dead!"

"One should not speak ill of those who have passed," Clara tactfully replied.

"You didn't spend much time with her. If I knew who killed her, I'd probably kiss him on the mouth."

"Marguerite!" said Horace in shock.

"Come now, don't pretend you don't feel the exact same thing. She was a pain in your backside and as tragic as a death might be, things suddenly get a whole lot easier for you."

Horace's eyes narrowed and Clara saw a flash, just for a moment, of the man who had found killing the creatures now beheaded and hanging from his walls great sport.

Clara looked at them both. "What do you mean?"

Marguerite lifted her glass to her lips. "Oh, nothing. Just fun and games with Nero inheritance rights. Cracking good decision to get that daughter of hers all engaged to your son, wot wot!" she said, mockingly at Horace.

But before Clara could inquire further, the sound of the door flinging open filled the house. They all ran out into the hallway.

Wesley stood there, drenched to the bone. He removed his borrowed hat and tried to brush off some of the water in a futile gesture.

"Well? Did you get the police?" asked Horace. "Are they on their way?"

Wesley shook his head. "I went as far as the bridge, but it is completely washed out. The river has risen and there is no crossing it. I'm afraid that we are on our own until this storm passes by. There will be no getting in or out until the water level drops. I wouldn't be surprised if the entire area floods."

Horace clasped his hands behind his back and tried to see a bright side. "Well, at least the house was built upon an elevation. Bedrock foundation. We shall be quite cozy and dry."

"And sitting ducks for whenever the murderer decides to show up again," pointed out Marguerite.

They all looked at one another. Horace took the key out of his pocket and went to the front door. He closed it and locked it. He then went to the parlor, shut that door and locked it, too.

He placed the key in a small pocket in his waistcoat meant for a watch. He patted it soundly and said, "Well, that is the only entrance to the parlor and I am the only one with a key. We shall just keep it locked until the police arrive. I shall make my rounds around the house since Gilbert is indisposed and ensure that all the doors and windows are fastened."

Wesley just stood by the front door, dripping sadly.

"Perhaps it is best if we were all to bed," Clara offered, going over to help Wesley remove his coat and hang the sopping mess where it would not ruin the floors. "I am sure things will look much different in the morning. There is nothing to be accomplished tonight besides fret. I advise all of you to finish your drinks. We shall lock ourselves into our rooms, just in case the murderer is still at large, and hopefully with the dawn, a course of action will present itself."

They all nodded in agreement. Marguerite went back into the dining room to pour herself another glass. Clara held her hand out to Wesley, inviting him to come with her.

They walked up the stairs and passed the bathing room. Clara went inside and grabbed several fresh towels for Wesley.

"Dry yourself off. I would hate for you to catch your death of cold when there seem to be so many other ways of catching death around this horrible home."

He laughed, even as he shivered slightly. "You are too kind, Clara."

"Not at all. You went out into that storm to save us all. Finding you a towel is truly the least I can do. Would you like me to come in and build up the fire in your room?"

"I can see to it," he replied. They stopped in front of Clara's door. It was open and she could see her bag waiting for her at the foot of the bed. He rested his hand upon her arm. "Let me examine your room to ensure it is safe before you go in."

She nodded, the frightful wisdom of his caution chilling her almost as deeply as if she was the one who went into the storm. She let him go first, but followed him into her chambers. Wesley looked beneath the carved double bed, opened up the wardrobe to look inside. He tested the windows to make sure that they were locked and made sure no one was hiding behind the curtains or door.

He gave her a nod. "It appears to be safe," he said.

"Thank you," she replied.

They stood there in silence for a moment. He reached out his hand to shake hers. "You are quite a brave woman, Clara. It is a shame such a tragedy had to strike. It was quite a pleasure to make your acquaintance and I am so sorry that our first memories of each other will be marred by such a terrible turn."

She smiled at him. "If such horrendousness had to happen, I must say that I am glad to have you here to take care of things. I hate to think how different this all would be if Norman or Horace were left to sort things out."

He nodded, and then returned her smile. He gave her hand one last squeeze before saying, "Now, lock your door behind me and promise that you shall not leave until dawn."

"You have my word, Wesley."

He began to walk out, and then paused, turning around. "I like when you say my name," he said, and then left down the hall.

Clara watched him until he disappeared into his own room, then shut her door and locked it. She paused, resting her hand upon its wood frame and whispered, "Heaven forgive me, but I like saying it, too."

Chapter Fourteen

Clara woke, shivering in her sleep. At first, she thought that one of the windows must have opened in the middle of the night. The room was as bright as if there was a full moon. But she heard the rain pelting upon the glass and realized that it was something else.

She turned onto her back and there was the girl, Minnie, the ghost who had haunted her in her room at home and somehow managed to follow her here.

Minnie stood in her unearthly light, her gauzy dress floating about her. Clara tried to still the fear which was making her heart beat fast. Minnie motioned for Clara to follow.

"You appeared earlier, Minnie, and someone died. I am frightened," Clara confessed.

But Minnie did not make any movement which suggested she heard Clara. Instead, she walked once more through the door, her hand returning to curl its single finger, calling Clara to follow.

Clara sat for a few moments. There was a murderer in this house. If Gilbert escaped, who knew what evil might befall her if she left her room. But the ghost's hand remained, calling her to leave her bed.

She closed her eyes and thought to herself that Minnie had led her to this house where all of these horrible things had occurred, but by the same token, Clara was the only one who could see her. If Minnie had anything to do with these terrible events, who knows what greater catastrophe would befall them all if she was not heeded.

And so, bravely, Clara took her robe from the foot of her bed and wrapped it around herself. She slipped her slippers onto her feet, unlatched the door, and followed after the ghost.

The strangest sense of déjà vu filled her, as the ghost wandered down the long, dark hall. She did not know if it was the memory of being led down her own dark hallway at home by this girl, or if she was aware of some other event which was to come. The heads of all the dead animals hung in the hall stared down at her accusingly, as if asking why she was not still in bed when the entire house slept.

But Minnie's reproach was far worse than these glassy eyed creatures, Clara decided. She crept down the stairs after the spirit, into the foyer, and then followed the glowing figure towards the library, the room where the party had originally gathered before dinner.

Minnie walked through the closed door. Clara tried to open it, but it seemed stuck, as if something heavy was pressed against it. She pushed and pushed with all her might. Finally, she cracked it enough to enter, but when she stepped in, she stepped onto something soft. She looked down in the dim light of the ghost's illumination and realized she was standing upon a housecoat sleeve.

The housecoat was being worn by one Norman Scettico. He was the heavy object blocking the door. His body was completely still and he did not move one bit as Clara opened her mouth and screamed.

Chapter Fifteen

In an instant, the house was awake and alive. Pounding feet raced down the stairs. Clara backed out of the library and pointed.

Wesley ran forward and gathered her up into his arms. She felt herself unable to stop trembling as she buried her face into his strong chest, his thin nightshirt soft against her cheek, the lapels of his velvet night robe giving her something to clutch to as she tried to will away the sight of the corpse.

Horace marched into the library as he put on his glasses. She heard him exclaim, "Great Scott!"

The others passed by and peered into the room.

"Well, I'll be damned," said Marguerite. "I guess that was one way to get him to shut up."

Clifford came over to Clara, patting her back. "There, there," he said, as if trying to coax her away from Wesley's comfort and into his own arms. "What a terrible fright you have had."

Horace was in a different mood. He exited and glowered at Clara. "Tell me what happened. Tell me every detail down to the last."

"I came downstairs," Clara gulped.

"Why? Why did you come downstairs?" demanded Horace. "We agreed everyone would stay locked in their room."

Clara looked up at Wesley, knowing that he was the only one who might understand what really happened. Instead, she just said, "I heard a noise. I thought I heard someone walking down the hallway and so I got up to investigate. I thought I heard them going into the library, so I followed. Only, there was something heavy against the door. I pressed and pressed. I'm afraid that it was Norman."

Wesley smoothed her hair, resting his cheek upon her forehead. "We'll get it all sorted. Don't you worry."

She realized that at this point, Norman would have been the one to accuse her of murder, but he was not there to shout such accusations. So instead, the entire room looked around at one another, unsure of what to do next.

Clifford shifted uncomfortably. "I'm sure you didn't kill him..." he finally said. "But the constable will want to know that we asked... You didn't kill him by any chance, did you? While you were sleepwalking or anything?"

"Oh for godssake," said Marguerite, rubbing her arms against the chill of the night. "Any idiot could tell that she did not kill him, then push him against the door, then pull the door open, and then turn into a blubbering mess. Obviously Gilbert escaped his room and is on the hunt. We need to find him before he finds us."

"I locked Gilbert's door with my own hands," Horace said, offended. "You and Norman saw me do it."

"We certainly did, but one of your witnesses is dead, leading me to believe that maybe things were not locked as tightly as you believed."

"Well, I never," said Horace, outraged at her accusation. "Let's go look in on Gilbert and we shall have our answer."

But Marguerite would not be cowed. "Well, let's!" she challenged.

Violet tried to take Clifford's arm, but he pulled away, more interested in keeping pace with Marguerite. So Violet trailed behind, forgotten and alone.

Wesley pulled a handkerchief from his pocket and dried Clara's cheeks as the party moved down the hallway towards the servant quarters.

"I must look a fright," Clara apologized.

"My dear, you look lovely as always," Wesley smiled. "Do you think you can stand much more of this?" he asked. "I could take you to your room to lie down."

She shook her head. "No, what if that fiend is still loose? I am far safer with this group than on my own." She stopped herself and then admitted what she really felt. "I am far safer with...you...than on my own."

He nodded and gently transferred Clara so that she could lean against him, wrapping his arm around her waist and resting her head upon him. "I shall keep you safe, dear Clara."

They slowly walked down towards the others. When they arrived, Horace was fiddling with his key ring, looking for the right one for the lock. "Damnable nuisance."

Clara should have extracted herself from Wesley's embrace at this point for reasons of modesty and good taste, but after such a night, she could not bear to stand alone. Instead, they leaned against one another for strength and waited.

Finally, the door opened. Horace bellowed as he walked into the room. "Gilbert! Gilbert, get up from bed you damnable fellow!"

But Gilbert did not stir. Instead, he lay upon the mattress, sleeping so soundly that he did not even move.

"Is he deaf?" asked Marguerite incredulously.

"I should say not!" said Horace. He strode over and shook his butler harshly. "Wake up, man!"

That's when Gilbert rolled from his side onto his back. His eyes were wide open. His throat was covered in blood, oozing from two puncture wounds in his jugular.

"Well, he is not deaf," said Marguerite.

Chapter Sixteen

H orace closed and locked the door behind him, in shock. "Three deaths in one night?" he said, incredulously. He repeated it again. "Three deaths. In one night. Under my very own roof."

"And the murderer does not appear to be Gilbert," remarked Marguerite.

Horace placed his hand upon the door, as if to assure himself that it was still solid and real. "How did someone get in there? They must have been a magician! To get into a locked room? To kill not one, but two men...?"

"Maybe it was Norman and then he fell and broke his neck?" offered Marguerite.

"No, no, that's not it," said Horace. He turned and looked at Clara sharply. "You said that you heard footsteps coming down the hall. What if that was the murderer! What if he lured Norman down just as he lured you down, and it was only your screams that kept the blaggard away! Dear, you may have saved us all! And yourself!"

Clara looked at Wesley and then at the faces of the others. "I don't believe I heard the murderer," she replied.

Horace did not seem pleased that she did not ascribe to his theory. "Well, then, you just tell me what you think happened."

"I don't know," Clara replied. "It was..." She realized that to hide the truth would make her look like she was lying, and in this situation, they might assume the worst. So she relented. "It was the same woman that I saw during the séance. She woke me and told me to come downstairs."

Horace's jaw dropped. "You're telling me some ghost told you to come downstairs and you just happened to stumble upon some room where Norman was lying dead?"

Clara cleared her throat uncomfortably. "Yes."

Wesley looked at her. "Really?" he asked, but she could see in his eyes that he believed her. Or at least that he wanted to believe her.

But it seemed that Horace had been pushed beyond that which his mind could accept. "Bah!" he said. "I have three dead people in my house. There might be ghosts, but there aren't GHOSTS. These aren't some haunted halls where dead women come to take a stroll. Don't tell me you believe this nonsense, Medium!"

Wesley held up his hands, as if asking him to provide a better answer if he had one. "There are stranger things in all the heavens than known to man."

"Don't go slaughtering quotations at me and expect me to take you seriously."

"Nice turn of phrase, Horace," Marguerite sighed.

"All I know is that there is a real, live, flesh and blood murderer still in this house and none of us are safe." Horace began pacing. "Perhaps not all of the staff went home. The storm was so terrible, perhaps someone used that as an excuse to stay. Perhaps they hid themselves here to take revenge upon me for... I don't know what! You never know with the help! They get the strangest notions in their head and soon, there is no reasoning with them! One day, they are asking for a raise in wages, the next they are luring young women out of their beds to murder them!"

"I was not murdered," Clara pointed out.

"A mere technicality!"

"It would make sense," Violet squeaked. "Someone here might bear a grudge against my mother. And it would make sense also to destroy the one man with the sense to decipher the clues scientifically. The one man who could figure it all out!"

"I could figure it out," said Clifford.

No one made a response in support and his statement hung awkwardly in the air.

Horace broke the silence by striding off, calling behind him. "Follow me!"

They all trooped along behind him, up the stairs, and towards the foyer. As they marched, Horace pulled a gun off of the wall in the hallway. He cocked it and said, "Loaded. Just like I left it. Come along then! Into the dining room!"

As soon as they were all inside, he locked the door and set about rallying their spirits. "See here, we are all in danger then. But never you fear! I shall protect us all. We shall remain hidden in this room until the storm breaks and we can go for help. There is strength in numbers and obviously, it is not safe for us to sleep alone. We shall all take turns keeping watch, except for the women of course. Delicate creatures and all."

Clifford pulled out two dining chairs. He sat in one and propped his feet up on the other. "Seems to me they could keep watch the same as any man," he grumbled.

"Quiet, boy. The women are free to do what they see fit. But it is a man's place to protect them and that is what we shall do," insisted Horace.

Marguerite pulled a derringer pistol out of the pocket of her robe and pointed it at the door. "Don't worry, Clifford, dear. I shall keep an eye out. Wouldn't want you to miss any of your beauty sleep."

"That was not what I was insinuating," Clifford tried to clarify.

"I don't think you were insinuating anything, you lily coward."

Clara pointed at the door at the far end of the library. "Excuse me. There are several entrances to this room, including one which goes into the room where Norman was murdered. And it appears to be open."

They all turned.

"Well, we know how the murderer got in," said Horace, removing his key and walking over to close and lock the doors.

"Wait," said Wesley. "Was that door open before?"

"What?"

"When you went in and looked at Norman's body, did you see this door open?"

They all stopped and looked at the room.

"I seem to recall it was closed," said Marguerite, her bright blue eyes flickering as she pieced together the memory. "And that's why it did not dawn on us that, of course, the murderer used it to enter and exit."

The open door stood there like an accusation.

"Well," said Horace, resolute but seeming as if he wanted someone to dissuade him. "I suppose we shall just have to go in and make sure our murderer is not lying in wait."

"You go and flush him out, father. I shall keep the women safe... make sure the murderer doesn't sneak around and get them while our backs are turned," said Clifford.

Marguerite rolled her eyes.

"May I borrow your derringer?" Wesley asked, hand outstretched.

Marguerite passed it over to him, handle first. "I call her Bessie."

"Thank you." Wesley gave Clara's hand a reassuring squeeze before he walked over to join Horace. "Shall we go inside?" he asked.

Horace nodded and like two men stalking prey in the tall grass, they crept towards the doors. They flanked the opening on either side and then, silently counting to three, they flung the doors open.

No one sprang out of the darkness at them.

"Can't see a blasted thing!" bellowed Horace. "How are we supposed to be able to see a damned thing without a light! Gilbert! Gilbert, bring a light!"

It was spoken out of habit, and it was only after the words left his lips that Horace seemed to realize what he said. Breaking the awkward silence, Clara rushed forward, taking a taper from the dining room table and going into the room to light the lamps upon the wall.

"What the devil!" said Horace.

The entire room had been tossed. Chairs were tipped on end. Books were ripped from their shelves. The skins were torn from the walls. A safe was behind one of them, and the wood around it bore deep scratch marks, as if someone had used an axe to try and gouge it out.

Marguerite peered inside. "You've redecorated, Horace."

Wesley carefully stepped through the room, looking in the fireplace, behind the chairs and the few curtains which remained hung in case someone was hiding. He lowered the derringer and returned it to Marguerite.

"Who would have done such a thing?" asked Horace, crouching down in horror to cradle the taxidermied head of his torn bear rug as gently as a broken lover.

"Obviously, there is something here that the murderer wanted," Wesley replied.

Clara stepped over to Norman's body, which had not been disturbed. She turned back to Violet. "There is something you said earlier... that the murderer most likely killed your mother because of a grudge, but then they would have killed Norman because he was the only one who could have solved the crime via powers of scientific deduction."

"I could solve it, too!" said Clifford, impotently.

"Quiet!" they all shouted back.

"What is inside of that safe?" Wesley asked Horace.

Horace stumbled to his feet and reeled across the floor to it. He spun the dial with tears in his eyes. "Nothing. Just legal papers. My marriage certificate.... the death certificate of Clifford's mother... the deed to the house."

"Wait!" shouted Clara.

"What?" asked Horace, wiping his dripping nose.

"The deed. The ghost led me to the deed of my house, which is why I came to see you in the first place, Horace!"

"I don't understand."

"There must be some connection," she reasoned out. "Why would the ghost lead me to a deed, and then all of this..." she pointed at the disaster of the room "...occurred, seemingly to get into a safe which contained a deed to your house."

"May we look at it, Horace?" asked Wesley, his hand outstretched.

Horace took a stack of papers out of the safe, riffled through them, and then handed the deed to Wesley. They all gathered round to look.

"There doesn't seem to be anything amiss," Wesley said to Clara. He passed it to her, to see if she noticed anything out of the ordinary.

"I should say that there is nothing amiss!" said Horace. "I just had it reviewed by my lawyer. I transferred ownership to your mother, Violet. It was to give her a place to live after your wedding."

"What?" she said, paling to a frightful shade of white. She turned to Clifford. "Did you know of this?"

The anger which rolled off of Clifford filled the room. "Yes. I told him that it was a foolish mistake. This house has been in the family for centuries."

"And it would have remained in the family, passing back to you and Violet, upon her death! Only you didn't marry that damned girl fast enough and now it all belongs to Violet and she isn't even your wife!" said Horace.

Violet gave a horrified cry at the callousness of his words. Horace jammed his hands into his pockets gruffly and said, "Yes, well, now you know, Violet. This house is yours."

"Why are you so anxious to rid yourself of this house?" Clara asked.

"I don't want to get rid of it at all!" Horace said. "But the damned tax collector will rip it out of my hands if I don't unload it. So, I was going to keep it in the family, so to speak."

"You could have just given it to me," whined Clifford.

"What? So you could lose it in gambling debts and set up some doxy in the country? Turn it into some pleasure palace of depravity? Not on my bear rug!"

Wesley took the deed back from Clara and crossed back over to the safe to replace it. He closed the door and spun the dials. "Well, if this is indeed the reason why the murderer struck, we now know. It stands to reason that he learned of this transfer and did not want the house to go to Hilda. We must take great care to watch over Violet tonight, in case he decides that she should not inherit, too."

Violet began trembling with fear. "I don't want to die!" she said. "I never wanted this house! Or this family! I never wanted any of this!"

Marguerite reached out and laced her fingers through Violet's hand, letting the poor girl lean upon her for strength. They made an odd pair, standing together, the protector and the weak. Suddenly Violet looked up, as if someone slapped her. "Are you wearing perfume?" she asked.

Marguerite looked startled by her reaction. "I have a scent mixed for me in Paris," she stammered.

Clara and Wesley exchanged glances. There were volumes not being spoken between these women. There was something about the perfume that upset them both.

Violet backed slowly away. "I have smelled that perfume before..." She walked back towards the dining room. "I must go sit down. This is all too much and I fear that I am beginning to imagine things."

"I shall come with you," offered Marguerite, almost apologetically.

"No!" Violet said. "Not you. You stay here..."

A coldness settled upon Marguerite as soon as Violet turned her back. Clara imagined a glint of danger in Marguerite's eyes.

But the moment was broken as Clifford sighed and dragged himself towards his fiancée. "Fine. I shall sit with you since you insist upon being parted from the group and heaven knows we can't have *you* killed before we get this house thing sorted."

"You are a real class act," Marguerite remarked drily. "What a lucky girl."

"This is all still conjecture," stated Wesley as Violet and Clifford left the room. "It could be nothing but coincidence. After all, we also have the murders of Norman and Gilbert. Gilbert was certainly not in the wrong place at the wrong time. He was locked in his room. Why would the murderer have taken the time to kill him?"

"Perhaps he saw too much?" said Marguerite. "He probably knows more about this household than anyone in this room."

"You can't trust anyone now days..." muttered Horace, picking through his broken trophies.

"But that still leaves Norman," pointed out Clara. "Perhaps he stumbled into the room at an inopportune moment, but why was he here in the first place?"

Wesley crossed and knelt beside the body. "He must have deduced something... he must have guessed something was amiss..."

"What is this?" asked Clara, crossing over to a chair.

"What?" Wesley and Marguerite replied in unison.

She reached beneath it. Tucked behind the foot was a crumpled piece of paper. She withdrew it and slowly spread it flat.

"It looks like a puzzle maze," she replied. "Almost like a child's game. All of the paths lead to the square in the center, but you can get to it four different ways. There are four arrows, one on each side of the square, all pointing in. It seems quite a beginner's level." She showed it to Horace. "Is this one of yours?"

He came over and looked at it. "Never seen it before in my life."

"I wonder how it got here..." Clara mused.

"Perhaps the murderer used it to get into the house," offered Marguerite.

"Or Norman brought it with him for some reason and he threw it aside so that the murderer would not find it," Wesley guessed.

Horace took it and folded it, placing it in his pocket with some finality. "Whatever it is, we shall save it for the authorities. Perhaps it is the calling card of our killer. The 'Maze Murderer' or some such rot." He looked about the room, the defeat in his eyes. "Can we not retire to the dining room? We really shouldn't be playing private investigator before the police have an opportunity to look at the crime scene. I find myself in need of a good, stiff drink," he admitted. "This really has been a terrible... most terrible... night..."

The sight of such a proud man so utterly destroyed was enough for all of them. Wesley nodded and the others silently agreed, retreating into the dining room, but not before Clara turned the knobs on all the lamps to extinguish them, plunging the library once more into darkness. Horace locked the door after they had all exited and sealed the room.

Chapter Seventeen

Violet rested her head upon the table, her arms folded to serve as her pillow. Her mousy sausage curls hid her face like the drapes of a weeping willow. Her shoulders shook softly with silent sobs. Clifford was pouring himself another drink and turned guiltily as the others entered the room.

"Did you get it all solved then?" he asked.

"No," snapped his father. "And if you are going to drink me out of house and home, why don't you pour me a glass, too?"

"Seems like I'm only drinking us out of Violet's new house and home, Father, since you saw so well to that," he slurred, casting an angry glance towards his fiancé.

"I hate you," Violet muttered quietly from the table. "I hate you all!"

Clara took Wesley's arm, needing contact with a rational, sane soul to steady her as the fighting escalated. It was as if no one else cared that a murderer might be near and three of their companions were now dead.

"Father," Clifford said, turning to Horace and swaying slightly. "Are you going to let her speak to me this way?"

"Quiet, boy!" Horace took the tumbler full of scotch from his son's hand and downed it. He waved the glass in his son's face. "You go find a nice corner to curl up in to sleep it off. In fact, all of you find nice corners to rest. I'll take first watch and when I come to hand it over, I want everyone bright-eyed and bushy-tailed and not falling asleep on the job."

Clifford bristled, red-faced and sweaty. "I shall not be tucked off into some corner like the women. I shall take the first watch like a MAN!"

Violet slowly sat up in her chair, as the sound of Clifford's voice caused something to snap. She looked at him with such hatred, such rage in her eyes. "No, you shan't."

"What?" he asked, turning towards her.

"Like a MAN? You are utterly incapable of protecting anything like a MAN. We would be better off just opening the doors and allowing the murderer to come take us!" she spat.

"Now, now, my sweet, shy Violet. You have been under such duress this evening," Clifford said, trying to calm her down. "It is no wonder that you are out of sorts. Go rest yourself."

"It is no use!" she shouted, hysteria taking over. "We are all going to die! Just like my mother died! Just like Norman died! Just like dear Gilbert died! And you think that you are capable of protecting us when men like that could not?" Her tiny, bird-like frame shook with rage.

"I assure you I am quite capable of fulfilling my manly duties," said Clifford, completely confused by her turn.

"Manly duties? Do you mean that in reference to being a man or to bedding whores and loose women? Because I know you are capable of only one of those things." Violet stood up and stepped forward, her eyes red and bloodshot, her face blotchy and puffed. "The only reason I even considered marrying you was because my mother said that I must. Well, now my mother is dead! I know it is not me that you seek to protect, but her!" she shouted, pointing at Marguerite. "I can see you look at her. I am no fool! It was her perfume I smelled on your clothes whenever you came near!"

"That is preposterous!" he protested.

"Really? Is it so? You thought that I was too stupid to notice? Well, now we are all going to die because you are no man. You are a coward! A liar! A cheat! The first moment we close our eyes, you will be sneaking kisses with Marguerite, meanwhile you will be too busy to notice when the murderer comes in and slits our throats as we sleep!"

"You are the fool!" he shouted back.

"I shall take this house and make sure you never step foot in it again!" she screamed.

"I AM a man!" he shouted back, ignoring her threats.

"Are you? Prove it! Prove to me what sort of man you are!" she challenged.

"You want me to prove what sort of man I am?" he responded.

"Yes!"

Clifford's eyes went wild. "Fine! FINE! I shall search this house from high to low until I find the murderer and kill him with my own hands! Then you'll see what sort of man I am!"

"Fine!"

"FINE!" he shouted, grabbing the gun from Horace and storming out of the room.

Clara turned to the group. "We can't just let him go out there by himself." She went into the hallway, calling "Clifford? Clifford! Come back!"

But Clifford was nowhere to be seen.

Chapter Eighteen

"He's gone!" Clara exclaimed to the room.

"He is gone? Where did he go?" said Marguerite, joining at her side. "He just stepped out into the hallway a moment ago. And now he is gone?"

Violet ran out after her, her anger faded into desperation. "Oh my word! What if I am responsible for his death! I never meant it! I was just angry! What if he dies because of me?"

She seemed once again on the verge of hysteria. Marguerite, seeing that Violet was not going to calm until the matter was resolved one way or another took her by the wrist and said, "He is not going to die. It has been all of two seconds. Most likely, he wandered off to hide under a bed somewhere. Come on. Let's go find him."

Wesley followed after as Marguerite and Violet began climbing the stairs. "We should come with you! There is strength in numbers."

Marguerite pulled out her gun and cocked it. "I assure you that we shall be just fine. How about you two turtledoves go search the downstairs while we go through the bedrooms?"

"Do you think that's safe?" Violet asked Marguerite.

"Clifford was always lousy at hide-and-seek. I'll take one side of the hallway while Violet takes the other, and I feel fairly confident we'll find him in under five minutes."

"But... I don't know if I can go with you... what if you're the murderer?" asked Violet.

Marguerite looked at her like she was an idiot. "If I was the murderer, I'd have killed Clifford first."

The entire room hung in silence.

"There is a bit of logic to it," Clara acquiesced. Violet seemed to agree and nodded her head before joining Marguerite at her side.

Wesley turned to Clara and asked, "Do you feel comfortable searching the downstairs with me?"

"Of course," she replied. "You are many things, Mr. Lowenherz, but you are certainly no murderer."

Horace raised his finger to interrupt them, fear filling the poor man's eyes for the first time that evening. "And what about me?" he asked.

Wesley replied, "You should stay here. Shout if he returns. You fearlessly faced the fiercest creatures from every corner of the globe. Of all of us, surely you can stand your ground against whatever monster we are dealing with on your own."

"I had several man-servants with me at the time..." Horace explained.

"Well, consider this the greatest hunt of your life." Wesley grabbed two swords off the wall. He tossed one to Horace who grabbed it by its hilt. Wesley unsheathed the other and held it out before him. He turned to Clara, "Shall we?"

Marguerite shouted, "Ready or not, Clifford! Here we come!"

Clara and Wesley made their way towards the basement, pausing to light a candelabra to bring with them. Slowly they crept down the stairs. Wesley took the front, ready to fend off any marauders, and Clara kept her eyes open for any dangers attacking from behind.

As they entered the large kitchen, Wesley stopped to light the gas lamps on the wall. "No need to go clunking around in the dark," he explained.

An ominous crack of thunder shook the house. Clara clutched his arm.

He smiled in grim amusement. "Really, for a woman who has seen three bodies tonight and the ghost of a fourth, I would not think you one to be frightened by a storm."

She held her hand to her heart, to cease its terrified beating. "It is strange the things that frighten a person. I suppose you are not frightened of anything, you who speak to the dead and can see beyond the veil."

Wesley paused for a moment, her words causing him hesitation. He spotted a hurricane lamp on the counter and lifted the glass to light the wick. Several moments passed before he spoke. "Fearful that I am about to disappoint you, I am afraid that poor Norman was correct. I am quite the quack. An outright fraud. A charlatan of the nth degree."

Clara stood stock still, her stomach dropping into her shoes with dread. "But I saw you at the vaudeville house! There was a message... from Thomas... it seemed as if he needed you to speak just to me..."

He shook his head sympathetically. "I try to keep such messages general enough that anyone could find meaning in them.

True, the message may have seemed to have been for you," he replied. "But it was from me. Not from beyond the grave."

"You cheat the grieving?" she asked, feeling as if her world might collapse.

Wesley pointed the burning taper at Clara. "No, I do not cheat the grieving. I might be a fraud, but I am not a cheat."

"Then why do you pretend to be able to speak with the dead?" she asked, begging for a reason to still believe in him.

Wesley leaned against the marble preparation counter, as if weighing how much he could trust Clara. Finally, he seemed to give up. "I have spent the past three years trying to get an audience with Horace. This whole mediumship nonsense was all just to get him into that parlor where I could try and get some answers from him."

"What?"

"You see, fifteen years ago, Horace lived in a different house. My sister, my fourteen-year-old sister, was working there as a housemaid. Something happened, and she was found dead in her room. The police quickly covered it up, swearing that she turned her hand against herself, but I know better. She never would have done that. I swear upon all that is holy, I believed that Horace killed her. That is why I am here. To find my sister's murderer."

Clara's mouth became dry, for she felt as if she knew the answer before it came out from her lips. "And what was your sister's name?"

"Minnie."

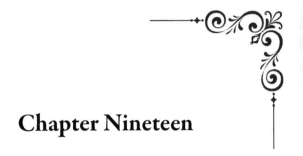

Chapter Nineteen

"Minnie," said Clara, disbelievingly. "You said to ask the ghost if her name was Minnie when we were in the parlor."

Wesley crossed the room to Clara and took her hands into his own. "You see, Clara, I am afraid that you are the true medium here. I thought to use parlor tricks to frighten an answer out of Horace. But instead, the horror has quite grown beyond any trick I know. I fear that perhaps he knew what I was up to and brought everyone here to kill them, just as he killed my sister."

"But I was holding his hand the entire time of the séance," said Clara. "He did not let go for a moment. He could not have snapped Hilda's neck."

Wesley rubbed his eyes. "Perhaps he used a false hand? Perhaps some other trick? But who else could it be? It is too great a coincidence."

"It must have been someone else," Clara replied. "There was no way for him to get from Gilbert's room back to the library to ransack it."

Wesley seemed torn. "And that is what troubles me the most. If I am wrong, if it is someone else... it means that all these years have been wasted and I have stepped right into a trap. Even worse, I wonder that if this ghost is true, if my sister is truly here tonight and has appeared to you, could it be that she is exacting her own revenge?"

Clara suddenly realized what Wesley was wrestling with. He was considering that his beloved sister might have the power to kill. She reached up tenderly to brush back Wesley's curled forelock, to comfort this poor grieving brother. "She would not seek revenge, dear Wesley. Of this I am sure. The events tonight have nothing to do with her. She is not some malevolent spirit. I feel almost as if she has come here to protect us, to warn us..."

He gripped her hand as if it were a lifeline. "But how do you know? What if, in order to save the people here, I must find some way to destroy my sister's ghost? What if Horace is indeed her murderer? Do I save him? Do I protect him from her?"

Clara could not stand to see him in such distress. She wrapped her arms around him, allowing the events of the evening to be her excuse to cross the boundaries into such intimacy. She held him as he had held her after she discovered Norman's body and let him lean upon her for support. "There, there," she said. "We shall cross that bridge when we come to it."

"I could not bear to think that my sister is resting so uneasily in the afterlife... that her death was so terrible she could not escape this earth..."

"Hush," she said, stroking his hair. "Hush."

When he had finally calmed, he looked down upon her, his eyes full of gratitude. He took her face in his hands and whispered, "If we are to die tonight, know that I have never met a woman finer than you, Mrs. Clara O'Hare."

The use of her full name, of the name that became hers when she married Thomas reminded her who she was and why she was here. She pulled away, breaking the spell between them. She could not. Not yet. "Come, there shall be time for such idle passings later. There is a murderer in this house and we must find Clifford before this monster kills again."

Wesley nodded grimly. She thought he seemed disappointed that she brought them both back to reality from that moment that was so pleasant between them, but there was no helping it.

He picked up the hurricane lamp and handed it to Clara. He then picked up his sword and they set to their task, searching room-by-room for Clifford, calling his name as they went through the pantry, the servant's quarters, the washhouse... but he was nowhere to be found.

"It is like he vanished into nowhere," said Clara. "He must be on one of the upper floors."

"What is this?" Wesley asked.

They had just entered the wine cellar, and Wesley pointed down at the ground. The dusty floor looked as if it had been disturbed by a door swinging out, only there was no door, only a wall of bottled wine. Wesley began feeling around the edges. "There must be a hidden entrance."

Clara held the lamp up high for Wesley so that he might see what he was doing. One by one, he lifted the bottles from their places to see if perhaps the weight of one might trigger the wall to move.

As Clara watched, she rested her hand upon the rack. Idly, her thumb began playing with one of the shelves. She felt a little knot, a rough spot that her finger began to work, and then, suddenly, there was a click and the wall swung out to reveal a passageway.

Wesley stepped back and looked at her. "Indeed, the finest woman I have ever met, Mrs. O'Hare."

She could not help the blush which she was sure was spreading across her face like wildfire and he seemed pleased that his admiration had such affect. But she did not allow herself to be distracted. Wesley entered the room and she followed close behind.

The doorway deposited them at the top of a set of stairs, which they crept slowly down until they reached a hallway made of old stones, worn from the years of hands and feet that had trod their way.

"This seems like a different house altogether," said Clara.

Wesley peered into the darkness. "So many of these homes were built upon old ruins and ancient burial grounds. I wonder if perhaps there was an old castle or fortress here, and the owners chose to borrow the foundation?"

"Horace did mention that this house was built upon an elevation..."

The darkness was oppressive; it seemed almost to have a life of its own. It was as if it was pressing upon them, trying to extinguish their flame. It was pitch black and no matter how hard she tried, she could see nothing beyond their lamp. The sound of water dripped in the distance. Clara hoped that the door had remained open at the top of the stairs. She could not imagine being trapped down here where there was no one to hear their cries for help.

It was then that she saw a glow that did not come from the light they carried. She felt the room plunge into cold as if doused in ice water. She grabbed onto Wesley's arm, shivering once again from both the chill and fear.

"What is it, Clara?" he asked.

Once more the ghost appeared, fading in like coming through a fog. Clara did not know whether to trust this spirit, or to prepare for her own death.

"It is Minnie," she said. "She is here."

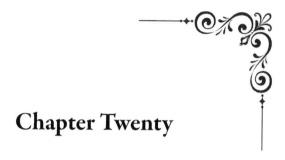

Chapter Twenty

"Minnie?" Wesley asked. "Where? Where?" He spun around looking for her, his voice filled with such a plaintive tone, as if he would give anything to see that which Clara could see so easily. But his sister remained a mystery. He gripped Clara's hand. "Please, tell her I love her and will seek justice for her murder. I will..."

Clara looked over. Minnie seemed torn, as if she would give anything to hear more of his words, but sensing some sort of danger or limit to their time. The mission won, and she held her finger to her lips, as if shushing him.

Clara placed her hand over Wesley's mouth. "She is motioning for us to keep quiet."

Wesley nodded and Clara slowly let him go, trying not to think about how his soft lips felt against her fingers, and that if they did not escape, it was the closest that she would ever come to knowing what they felt like.

Minnie motioned to Clara to follow with her slow, trance-like movements. Clara took Wesley's hand and led him after the ghost. The hallway was a warren, and this secret basement could have easily extended the entire length of the house. They wound through the maze like hallways.

"It would not be unexpected to run into a minotaur in these walls," muttered Wesley.

Minnie turned and gave him a glare, and for once, Clara thought he was perhaps lucky that he could not see his sister.

The hallway finally stopped at a large, wooden door with iron bands across the boards. A shape gouged from its surface, marring the symbol or decoration beyond recognition. Wesley squeezed Clara arm, as if to infuse her with a bravery neither of them felt, placed his hand upon the black, metal ring which served as a handle, and pulled.

The door opened upon a large square room. Cautiously, Wesley looked inside before stepping in, then motioned for Clara to follow. The room seemed almost a mirror image of itself, each wall the same as the wall opposite it fitted with four matching doors. It would have been easy to get confused and walk through the wrong one.

"It is like that maze drawing we found in the library," Clara remarked. "Do you think it could have been not a puzzle, but a map?"

"Perhaps you are right," said Wesley as he crossed to the opposite door and pushed against it. It would not open. "But why four doors?" Wesley asked. "This room is hidden deep in the center of a maze, as if to protect whatever was at its heart, but four doors would be impossible to defend. You would have to fight four directions."

In the center of the room was a raised square platform of granite. In fact, the entire room seemed as if had been carved from a single piece of rock. Clare looked closer and could see no seams between the walls and the floors, and the floor and that platform. Carved into the center of the platform was a hole. A heavy stone lid, which looked like it would have fit perfectly over it, was pushed to the side. A large metal chain with an open padlock pooled around it, as if someone might have once tried to lock something or someone inside, and some foolish person undid that good deed.

"Perhaps it was not about keeping something safe inside, but a four part trap defensible on all sides, to ensure it did not get out." Clara gripped Wesley's arm tightly and whispered, "What is stronger than a man and can snap a grown woman's neck with no one seeing? What creature leaves two fang marks in its dead? And sleeps in a coffin within a square room?"

"Horace..." Wesley said.

"What?" asked Clara, confused.

Wesley ran his hand over the back of his head, smoothing his auburn hair mindlessly as he thought. "This is Horace's house. This is Horace's basement. Think on it! He is a man who loves the hunt, almost like a beast he tracks his prey. He has brought us here, all of us. He dismissed every servant that could have born witness to this night and killed the only one remaining. He ensured that we were stranded, without any hope of actually reaching the police. He is our monster! And we left him alone by himself! And now he is free to stalk all of us at his leisure!"

"But he is just a man!" Clara insisted.

"Are you sure?"

"Do you mean to suggest he is not a man?"

"We must get out of this house," said Wesley, leading Clara back towards where they just came.

"But what is he?" she insisted.

Wesley opened his mouth to give words to the horrible truth they were both thinking, but before he could say anything, they both heard a woman's scream echoing through the stone.

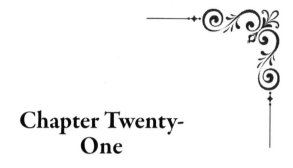

Chapter Twenty-One

"That was Marguerite!" Clara cried.

"Quick! We must save her before he claims another victim!" said Wesley.

They both made towards the door to dash out the way they came, but suddenly, it swung shut on them.

"No!" said Clara, running to the handle and trying desperately to unlatch it. "It is locked from the outside!"

But then the door on the opposite side flung open.

Clara looked back at Wesley and then notice that Minnie was trying to get her attention. The ghost had brought them here. They had no other choice but to trust her again.

The second door shut and a third door opened.

"It will close," Clara muttered. "This way!" she cried. She ran towards the fourth and final door and was ready to leap through as the third door slammed closed and it opened. Wesley was behind her in close pursuit.

But this door led to a set of stairs instead of to another winding hallway. They paused for only a moment before Wesley placed his hand on the small of Clara's back and propelled her up. There was no other way to go.

The stairs seemed to travel inside the walls of the house. There was a small hole in the wall and light was shining through it. Clara paused.

"Really! We must get to Marguerite!" Wesley urged.

But she hushed him. "You can see into the library through these holes. Poor Norman is lying right there in the middle of the floor." Clara then felt the wall beside her. "And look! This is a door! This is how our murderer got in!"

Wesley looked in through the holes, too. "By gum, you're right! Look at all that you can see! Who knows how long we were being spied upon! Or by whom!"

"This home hides many wicked secrets," Clara said.

"We never should have come. If I had any idea the sort of trap that we were walking into..."

Minnie's ghost had disappeared. Clara felt the warmth return and at once she was quite hot from the exertion. She wiped her brow. "Your sister is gone. This is what she wanted us to see. This house and that square room."

They were interrupted once more by another scream. It sounded like it was coming from above them.

"Violet!" they both exclaimed. They began running as fast as their feet would take them, up more stairs and deeper into the walls. They paused every chance they had to peer into the holes, hopeful that one of them would reveal the whereabouts of the two ladies, but also fearful of what they might find.

Finally, they could go no further. The hallway dead ended into a door and they had not seen the girls in any of the rooms they passed.

"Dare we go out?" asked Clara.

Wesley gripped the handle of his sword. "We have no other choice."

They both placed their hands upon the door, and in one movement, they pushed and ran.

Standing there in the middle of the hallway was Clifford, Violet, and Marguerite involved in a heated argument.

Clara and Wesley looked at one another, unsure of what was going on.

"I told you, Violet, I shall love you forever!" said Clifford, pleading with the young heiress.

"You only ever loved me for my money, Clifford!" wept Violet. "And now that Maman is dead, you will not touch my inheritance!"

"You said the same thing when you swindled your way into my pocketbook, Clifford!" shouted Marguerite. She raised her derringer and pointed it at his forehead. "I swear to the lord above, I would do all of womankind a favor if I killed you where you stood!"

"No!" screamed Violet, flinging herself protectively in front of Clifford, terrified by this violent turn.

Wesley ran forward. "Please! Have you all taken leave of your senses? There shall be no more talk of killing anyone tonight! We have had quite enough of that."

A roll of thunder crashed.

"Please! Please! We must all get out of this house before Horace kills us all!" Wesley shouted. His voice cut through all the chaos and stopped everyone in their tracks.

"What did you say about my father?" asked Clifford stepping forward.

Wesley explained. "We found a secret room beneath the house. We know what he is. And all our lives are dependent upon us escaping before he figures out that we know what we know!"

"You are talking madness! My father is the murderer?" said Clifford incredulously. He turned to the two girls who had been close to ending him just moments before. "I am going downstairs. I shall get to the bottom of this!"

"No!" cried Wesley and Clara, reaching for him, but he was too fast and dodged their fingers. He ran down the stairs. Clara and Wesley made chase, following close on his heels, ready to provide whatever protection they could.

They all entered the dining room at the same time and they all saw the same thing at the exact same time, too. Horace. Dead. Two puncture wounds to his neck and his face as pale as pale can be.

"We were wrong," said Wesley, breathlessly. He wiped his forehead, as if his mind was reeling. He turned to Clifford and pointed. "You! You were the only one who was by himself and could have come back to kill him! You are the monster!"

Clifford backed slowly away, his face twisting in rage. He raised his father's gun and pointed it straight at Violet's heart.

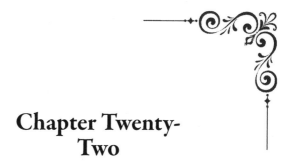

Chapter Twenty-Two

Violet shrieked, her high, feminine voice squealing at top pitch. Frantically, she began to panic. "I knew it was you! I knew you wanted to kill me! I knew you were desperate for my money!"

Clifford began to laugh maniacally. "It is not yours! It was never yours! This engagement was a sham! I would never marry you!"

Violet turned to Wesley. "He is going to kill me just like he killed everyone else!"

Wesley, arms outstretched in peace, tried to inch closer to Clifford. "Put the rifle down, Clifford. Is this really what you want to do?"

Clifford swung his rifle off of Violet and towards Wesley. "Don't you take another step closer! You're all mad! MAD I tell you! And I am getting out of here alive if I have to kill every one of you!" He pulled back the hammer and took aim.

And in that moment, Marguerite, with her small derringer, fired. It hit Clifford in the chest. He clutched at his heart, swung and fired, hitting her in the stomach.

They both fell to the floor, bleeding.

And that is when Violet began to laugh.

It was a bone chilling sound.

Slowly, daintily, she picked her way over Marguerite's fallen body and made her way to Clifford. She crouched down, fear shining in his dulling eyes. She reared back her head, and as she did, she sprouted four fangs where her canines should be, and plunged them into his neck.

Clara screamed as Violet descended upon him to feed with an animal-like lust.

"Violet?" said Wesley, unable to believe his eyes. "She's the one?"

But what they saw before them brooked no argument. Wesley raised his sword and ran towards her, ready to do whatever it took to stop her, but she never gave him a chance. The tiny woman flew from Clifford's now still body and knocked the sword out of Wesley's hand like it was nothing but a toy. With her other arm, she sent the back of her hand across his face. His head made a terrible sound as he fell and it hit the ground.

Clara made a dash for the sword, but Violet paid her no mind. By the time Clara turned, the sword in hand, Violet and Wesley were gone without a trace.

Clara stood, her breath heaving against her tightly bound corset. She did not know where they went, where to give chase, or what to do.

She looked up at the ceiling of the room and said, "Minnie? Minnie are you here?"

There was nothing but silence. The cold did not come. Clara felt lost and alone. Panic rose in her throat, thinking of what Violet might do to Wesley and that she was powerless to help. She could not let him die! Not when she was just beginning to believe that there might be someone else to walk beside her in this life. She could not lose another piece of her heart.

"Please, Minnie!" she pleaded.

"Who are you talking to?" came a weak voice.

Clara turned to see Marguerite staring at her. Blood was pooled all about where she lay, and yet, for some reason, she was still alive.

Frantically, Clara looked around the room for something to staunch the bleeding. There was a napkin on the dining table. She grabbed it and ran to Marguerite's side. "Wesley's dead sister."

Marguerite winced in pain as Clara pressed the cloth against the wound. "Tell her that I am on her side, too."

"What do you mean?" asked Clara, taken aback. "You do not think I am delusional?"

"Norman and I are... were... with the local authorities. *Special* local authorities. We both knew that something was amiss... Too many young girls have perished in the household of Horace Oroberg for it to be a coincidence..."

"But it wasn't him!" said Clara. "It was Violet. She is not what she seems. She ate the throat out of Clifford there." She pointed to his lifeless body, his eyes staring wide open in shock and surprise.

But, again, Marguerite was not surprised. "I knew... I knew at the end it was her... I waited because I wanted to make sure... it is my fault... she could smell my perfume... I knew..."

She began to fade, her words becoming weaker. Clara grabbed a goblet from the table and dribbled water into her mouth. Marguerite revived for just a moment, gasping out her words. She clutched at Clara's dress. "You must take my gun... It will not dispatch Violet, but it may slow her down... You must take the sword and cut off her head... It is the only way to stop her..."

Clara looked down at the sword in her hand. "You ask too much!"

"It is the only way to save your Wesley..."

Clara paused, and then nodded, rising to her feet.

"Tell him, when you get a chance, that you love him. Life is too short to leave such things unsaid."

And then Marguerite's eyes closed and Clara knew she was on her own. But not quite on her own...

She whet her lips and said again, this time insistent, "Minnie, your brother is in grave danger. Your brother, whom you love... and of whom I... I have begun to feel things that I have not felt for a long time... He needs your help. Please, Minnie. Do not hide yourself from me. I need your help to save him!"

The room remained the same.

"Please, Minnie!" Clara begged. "I love him!"

Marguerite's lips began to move, but not from her own power. Her eyes were closed and her body lifeless, but the voice which came out filled the house. She said, "I am coming."

Slowly the room began to chill. The gas lights began to dim. The china upon the table began to shake and the goblets dance upon its surface until they tipped over.

Clara waited, terrified as a rabbit facing down a wolf. The energy in the room was not kind. It was filled with violence and anger.

"Please, Minnie!" she pleaded. "Direct your anger not towards me, but towards that creature who has taken your brother hostage. Show me the way and I shall go to him! I shall do whatever it takes to save his life!"

The window farthest from her burst. And then the window beside it exploded, too. A great wind blew through the house, causing all of the lamps to sputter out. It raged against Clara, wrapping her nightgown around her legs and pushing her towards the hallway. It would not allow any protest.

The wind continued, knocking the trophies from the walls and breaking the mirrors. The head of a boar flew across the hallway with such force, the tusks impaled themselves into a wall. The doors opened and slammed shut as Clara passed, and she knew that if she lost courage and tried to run to a room for safety, the door would close on her and cut her in two. The entrance to the basement flung open and a mighty wind roared up the stairs, striking her in the face. It was as if two forces of nature were battling it out to see who would allow Clara to pass.

The upstairs wind grasped her, feeling as if a giant hand had wrapped itself around her waist, and it hurled her down the steps. Her feet could barely keep up with its speed. She could hear the opposing wind howling around the protection of this mighty force.

She placed her elbow over her brow to try and keep her face safe from the debris. A rat flew past her cheek, the wind taking no prisoners. She looked ahead and saw the glow she knew now was Minnie. She prayed that she was not making the gravest mistake of her life. She bent over and followed, and tried to keep up.

They wound their way through the warren of hallways, Minnie's light ahead the only thing to illuminate Clara's way.

As the wind buffeted against her, there were a few moments in which she almost lost track of Minnie, in which she was almost plunged into the darkness, and she could feel that there were things waiting for her outside of Minnie's light. She could hear their snuffling and the sound of their claws upon the ground. It was like her nightmares, except this time, they were real. She wondered if Horace ever had known as he was out hunting on the savannah that the most terrible creatures were, in fact, right below his feet.

Clara pushed on, refusing to surrender to the darkness, refusing to let the terrors beyond grab a foothold. She had faced them again and again, night after night, and realized it was, perhaps, all practice for this. She would not go down without a fight. She caught up with Minnie and though exhausted, she pushed on, thinking only of Wesley and that she must save him from whatever horrors Violet had in store.

And then she saw the doorway. Minnie waited for her in front of it, her eyes filled with rage, but also with pleading.

Clara stopped to catch her breath. She did not know whether to carry the revolver or the sword into the room. She was no experienced warrior. She was only a foolish widow, who followed the clues set by a ghost. Fear caused her teeth to chatter and her hands to shake. Minnie's light was beginning to fade, and Clara knew that if she did not go in before Minnie disappeared, she would have no defense against the creatures of this maze.

And then a quiet sense of peace and resolve descended upon her. She would either save this man she loved, or would be sent to join the man who was waiting for her beyond the veil. There would be no losing. Either outcome would bring her to happiness, and she knew that she was now ready to face that. Fear no longer held any power.

She opened the door.

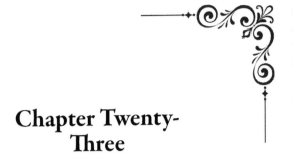

Chapter Twenty-Three

The lid had been slid back onto the coffin, sealing it closed, and Wesley lay upon it. He was chained by his hands and feet in a giant X, his limbs pointing to the four corners of the room. Candles were lit and placed in a circle around him. Clara almost sobbed from relief. He was alive.

But that relief did not last for long, for Wesley cried, "Run! It is a trap!"

The door behind her slammed shut and Clara felt a strong foot kick her in the small of her back, sending her sprawling upon the floor. She flipped over to see her attacker.

Violet, dear sweet Violet, was horribly transformed. Her large, doe-like eyes were now red. Her fingernails were like claws. Her clothes were torn and stained with the rust color of her fiancé's blood.

"Tricky, tricky, little girl," she hissed as she crawled slowly towards Clara. Clara scrambled to her feet, holding the sword in both hands before her.

"You thought to hide from my children of the square, hide from the darkness that only wishes to welcome you into its eternal embrace."

"Why are you doing this, Violet?" Clara asked. She jumped to the side with a scream as Violet tried to rush her. "Why?"

Violet looked up, almost surprised that Clara had avoided her grasp. She spun, training her eyes on Clara once again. "You have learned a trick or two from those ghostie friends of yours."

"I have learned nothing, Violet. Just let us go. We shall leave you here in peace. Just let us leave."

"No, no, my dear." Violet looked over at Wesley. "This naughty trickster tried to pretend that he could see ghosties, too. But I see now he does not hold the power. He shall die for his lies!"

"But I do not lie! I can see them! Let him go and take me instead!"

Violet hissed. "I shall take you whether you like it or not!"

She leapt again at Clara and Clara managed a half-hearted swing with her sword, which Violet easily avoided.

"You come here with a sharp little knife, thinking you can harm me?" she laughed.

"I do not wish to harm you, Violet!"

"Violet!" shouted Wesley from where he lay bound and helpless. "Why don't you tell her the harm you were planning to do? Tell her how you killed my sister all those years ago. How you killed all the people in the house searching for just one that could talk to the spirits beyond the grave! Tell her how you will use her powers to lock all the souls who pass away from this moment forward in Purgatory and forever deny them their eternal rest! Tell her how you will lock her in this tomb and drain her strength to grant you immortal life! Tell her all the reasons why she should fight to her dying breath to bring you down!"

Violet hissed. "Quiet, you! Think that your words can turn the tide? I shall have my way with you and you shall be my dinner when I am through!"

But Wesley's words had their intended effect. Clara realized what was at stake. And with Violet distracted, she fired a single shot from Marguerite's derringer.

The bullet struck Violet's shoulder, causing her to turn away from Wesley with a hiss. She flew towards Clara and this time she did not miss. She struck Clara's wrist, knocking the sword from her grasp and it went clattering harmlessly to the floor. Clara was left holding nothing but the empty derringer, and with another blow, Violet rid her of that, too. Wesley struggled against his bonds, as if somehow he could find the Herculean strength to break free from his iron shackles. Violet struck Clara across the face with the back of her hand, and then followed up the blow with a raking slap from her other palm.

Clara was thrown to the ground. She clutched her cheek, feeling a stinging pain and then sticky warmth upon her fingers. She looked up at Violet, unable to comprehend how such a frail girl could be so strong.

Violet licked the blood which her claws had drawn and smiled as if tasting some divine delicacy. "I can feel your power even in this drop." Her eyes fixed upon Clara. "I must have more!"

She flew at the woman, and Clara rolled to the side, barely escaping as Violet struck the ground beside her violently. She did not even pause. Violet scrambled like a dog in a bull pit and came after Clara again. Terrified, Clara tried to crawl away. She felt an iron grip wrap around her ankle. Clara kicked and kicked, calling for Wesley through her tears, "Help!"

And he could not. He strained, every inch of his body trying to get to her. "No!" he cried in vain. "CLARA!"

Clara caught Violet in the face with her heeled shoe, the impact making a sickening crunch. Violet screamed in anger, but that did not stop her from reaching out and grabbing Clara's other foot. She hung on and Clara could not shake her.

Clara dragged their two bodies across the floor, using her elbows and arms to gain inches. She was going to die, she realized. She was going to die, and for all the times she had longed for death, she finally realized, without a shadow of a doubt, that she did not want to.

She stretched, and with the tips of her fingertips, she touched one of the candles. She pulled it from the circle surrounding Wesley, and with all her might, she threw it upon the creature. Violet let go, screaming, as her dress caught on fire and it went up as if she had been doused in kerosene.

Clara took the moment of Violet's distraction to run to Wesley, tugging futilely at his bonds. "I cannot free you!" she cried.

"Leave me!" he shouted. "You must end her!"

Clara turned around to see Violet screaming, her dress now a roaring blaze. Her skin was charred and bubbling, but as it sloughed away, it revealed that the face of Violet was merely a disguise to hide her true form.

What was beneath was like tanned leather, hide and scales rather than skin. Her teeth were rows of fangs. Her eyes were red. Horns sprouted from her head and the voice which came out was not that of a young girl.

"Think that you can stand against me?" it roared.

Clara could not help the scream which tore its way through her throat. She ran to the far end of the room, as far away from this creature as possible, as if somehow she might find some place to hide within the barren tomb. She pressed up against the wall as the creature grew closer, its voice so strong that it cause the very ground to shake. The room became hotter as the thing continued to burn.

She needed to escape. Panic and fear coursed through her body. She looked over at the door, realizing there were only seconds before the monster was upon her.

And that was when Clara remembered the map which Norman had carried showed four entrances with arrows pointing in. Wesley said that four entrances would be terrible to defend, but perfect for an invading attack. What if the maze was built not to confuse people and keep them away, but to keep this creature trapped? What if there was something out there that could help.

Clara ran to the door closest to her and pushed it open. Wind filled with the screams of a thousand tortured souls blasted into the room. She leaped out of the way, trying to get out of the stream. The creature began to laugh, calling the wind towards it, letting it wrap around its arms and legs lovingly. "You think that letting in my minions will help you defeat me?"

Clara stood in horror, not sure of the damage which she had done. She needed balance for this wind. She needed the opposite arrow as drawn upon the paper, a force which was equal to this force. She needed to counteract what she unleashed. Not knowing if she was about to make it better, or worse, she dodged passed Violet, feeling the searing heat of the creature. She reached the door on the other side, and flung it open. Immediately, another hurricane gale swept into the room, but this one was filled with the sound of tinkling chimes, and then a roar of anger. It smashed into the wind swirling around Violet and ripped it away, turning it into a tornado which now hung above Wesley.

It was not enough, Clara thought. She needed to shift the wind once more. She needed to trap the demon in the center of this force. She looked at the two remaining doors. If this room was about balance, about using two perfectly matched opposing forces to hold something in the middle, one door would bring in Violet's creatures of the dark, the other door would bring in the powers that could vanquish them. Whichever door she chose next would tilt the balance.

She looked at Violet.

The creature was edging around the storm, trying to get to where Clara stood. She saw that time was running out and a decision must be made. There was the door she had entered, the one which required Minnie's protection and guidance to survive. And then the other.

It was a guess, a risk, and she prayed that she was not making a terrible mistake, but she ran to the unknown one and opened it.

A gale poured into the room, almost knocking Clara off her feet, but it did not contain the screams of horror. Instead, it was a deathly cold, and as Clara looked up, she saw that mixed in with the wind and dust and debris, was a glowing light.

"Minnie?" she whispered.

The wind slammed into the tornado and pushed it against the far wall.

Clara picked up her sword, and with great hacking strokes, came after the creature, swiping and knocking away its claws. Slowly, inexorably, she backed it across the room, her will to live stronger than any of the creature's strategy. The wind aided her, sucking the demon back, back, back until it backed itself into the tornado and was caught within the swirling wind.

The creature screamed as it tried to claw its way out from this elemental cage. Clara lowered her sword, and with fierce determination, strode over to the final door and opened it.

Once more, the wind swept into the room, this time bringing with it all the creatures the demon had laid as traps within the maze. They joined the maelstrom, spinning around the thing that was Violet. The wind picked the creature up and elevated it above where Wesley lay shackled. Clara thought that if it had been she, and not Wesley, trapped on that stone, this was where the final moment of the creature's spell would have taken place to free it for eternity.

But that was not how events had transpired.

Clara climbed onto the tomb, standing in between Wesley's legs as the tornado held the creature for her. She raised the sword above her head. The silver edge gleamed. And in that moment, she saw the face of Minnie. Wesley's sister held the head of the creature back for her, baring Violet's neck so that Clara would have a clear shot.

"Thank you, Minnie..." she said.

With a mighty two-handed stroke, Clara cut through the wind. She felt the edge of her blade strike the creature. She felt its roar vibrate the hilt of her blade. She felt herself cutting through the sinews of its neck, passing through as if it was melting beneath her touch.

And then the head fell off the shoulders, rolling onto the ground.

And that was when the world exploded.

Chapter Twenty-Four

"Clara? Clara, darling?" came a gentle voice.

At first, she was only aware of the aching pain of her bones, as if she had been thrown from a horse or taken a terrible fall. But then she felt the strong arms around her, gentle hands stroking her face and hair, inviting her to return.

She slowly opened her eyes, blinking in the dim candlelight. Wesley's face floated above her. He was holding her close to his chest, cradling her as delicately as a child. His strong jaw was clenched, his brow furrowed. She wanted to find out what caused him such distress, to soothe away his trouble. And then she realized that he was worried about her.

She was tired, so tired, she wanted nothing more than to stay in his arms forever, but she gave him a weak, reassuring smile.

This one little movement broke the artifice of control that Wesley had been trying to maintain. He collapsed, leaning his lips upon her forehead and whispering, "Oh my dear, oh my dear... I thought I had lost you..."

She felt his breath shudder in ragged gasps. She felt him try to wrestle control of his emotions and fail. She wanted to murmur to him not to weep, that she was here now, to be with him, and that the danger was finally gone. She lifted a hand to his face, resting her palm against his cheek. He took it in his, pressing it against his lips and holding onto it tight, so tight, it seemed as if he thought it was a lifeline lifting him from beneath the waves to the safety of the shore.

"You are free..." she whispered.

"The manacles disappeared the moment the monster did," he replied. "There is nothing more to fear."

"We are safe?"

"Because of you, my darling," he replied, placing her hand upon his heart, so that she might feel its beat. "All because of you."

"And the creature?" she asked.

"Gone. Gone and with it, all its minions, sent to the pits of hell, never to be seen again. You alone vanquished it. You alone saved us all."

He looked at her, his face a conflict of emotion. There were words upon his lips that he seemed frightened to say. He seemed to be searching for something, some sign, that to open himself to this possibility, he would not be rebuked, that he would not ruin this moment, that he would not destroy the perfection of just he and she at the start of the world.

So instead, Clara said it. "I could not leave you," she confessed. "I did not wish to live if I knew that there was not a chance of you being at my side."

Her words seemed to cause time to stop. She felt his heart skip a beat, and then double its pounding. She felt his breath fill his chest in a mighty sigh of happiness. He looked down upon her, his dark, brown eyes filled with tears of joy. Slowly, taking each moment so that she could stop him or pull away, he closed the distance between the two of them, placing his lips softly upon hers to seal her confession with the tenderest of kisses.

That kiss chased away all the pain in her bones until the aches were just a memory. That kiss chased away the pain in her heart and washed over the wound Thomas left there. It soothed its festering like a healing balm and mended it with Wesley's love. Wesley gripped her tighter, as if never wanting to let go, and she clung to him, wanting him to know that she finally found home.

He lifted away from her, his face awash in disbelief. Clara almost laughed. It seemed as if, despite demons and magic and otherworldly horrors, he could not think *this* was true.

"Come, my darling," she whispered. "Let us leave this terrible place. We have the rest of our life to begin."

He kissed her once more, and then slowly helped her to sit. He crouched, placing her arm around his neck, and lifted her to her feet. Her knees buckled beneath her, unable to stand, but he caught her, letting her use his strength for as long as she needed.

"I cannot walk," she said, realizing that she was too weak to support herself.

He smiled. "Then I shall be your legs." He reached down and swept his arm beneath her knees, lifting her as easily as a feather, and carried her out of the room into the world that waited for them beyond.

Chapter Twenty-Five

They sat in the carriage, the sights of the city passing by the window. It was a place that seemed to have existed a lifetime ago, and not just the twenty-four hours which had passed. Clara leaned her head against Wesley's chest, his arm wrapped around her, propriety be damned.

They had returned upstairs to the house to find that Marguerite was still alive, and that she had crawled over to the telephone. She was slumped against the wall, the receiver dangling by her head. She gave a weak salute. Whatever force was banished upon Violet's defeat had also broken the storm and restored use of the phone. Marguerite had been able to ring the constable and the entire police force was on their way by the time that Clara and Wesley emerged.

Though faint and pale from the loss of blood, Marguerite seemed in good spirits. "The damned bullet seemed to have hit one of my stays." She pointed at the metal ribbing of her corset. "I have never been so grateful for this horrible contraption."

Wesley deposited Clara upon a chair in the hallway, close to where Marguerite sat collapsed, and ran off to find some sort of bandaging to aid the injured woman. After he left, Marguerite leaned forward and asked, "So? Did you get her?"

Clara nodded and Marguerite leaned back, as if finally she could rest. "Good. Good..."

"What was it?" Clara asked.

"We don't entirely know," Marguerite said.

"We?"

Marguerite nodded. "This is not the first time such a creature has appeared. They prey off the sadness of others. They seem to look for people that no one would seem to miss if they disappeared. Norman and myself have been hunting them for years."

Clara looked over at the library where Norman's body was hidden. "I am so sorry for the loss of your friend."

Marguerite waved her off. "He was a damned pain in the ass." Her face softened just a bit though. "He would not have wanted to go any other way. Far better to be taken in battle than crippled and gray and trapped with the memories of all the things we've seen." She glanced at Clara. "That said, I shall be looking for a new partner, if you know of anyone."

Clara did not say anything, just gave her a smile, and the two of them sat in silence until Wesley returned.

As the cab pulled in front of Clara's house at the end of the garden square, a bewildered look crossed Wesley's face.

"What is it, my love?" she asked.

"You live here," he replied.

She gazed up at him, wondering why it seemed so strange. "Indeed. Why?"

"This was the home where my sister was killed," he said.

Of course Minnie, his sister, was the girl who died in this home. Minnie was the death she had been warned of when she purchased the building. In the chaos of what they had been through, she had been so anxious to get home, and Clara had not been thinking of Wesley's ties to this place.

"Are you all right?" she asked tenderly.

He nodded, his thoughts still far away. "Of course. I passed this house so many times after her death. It always reminded me of her. And to think that her spirit was waiting here, the entire time, needing someone who could see her." He stroked Clara's hand and returned to her with a tender smile. "I am so glad it was you."

"She led me to you," Clara said. "It was she that protected me through the maze and helped me to defeat Violet. She has been looking out for you, even though you did not know it."

Wesley kissed Clara's forehead, resting his lips in gratitude for those few simple words, as if finally, he was at peace. He got out of the carriage and helped Clara out. The cab driver set her bags upon the sidewalk and Wesley picked them up, escorting her to the door.

"My butler and housekeeper lived there at the time, too," she said. "Perhaps you would like to come in and speak with them of her memory."

"What are you talking about?" asked Wesley.

"They said that they served on staff when the murder happened," Clara replied.

Wesley set the bags down before the door and took her hands in his. "Clara, this house has sat empty for years. The entire household staff was killed along with her that terrible night."

The front door opened and Mr. Willard walked out. Clara looked at him, truly looked at him, as if seeing him for the very first time. He held his fingers to his lips and Clara suddenly understood.

"I must have been mistaken," she replied to Wesley.

He looked at the open door and remarked, "Your door seems to have a broken latch."

"I shall have Mr. Willard look to it as soon as I get inside," she replied, then leaned over and placed a kiss upon Wesley's cheek.

Wesley smiled, his love warm as the spring sun shining down upon her. He lifted her fingers to his lips. "I shall see you tomorrow?"

"Tomorrow, if not sooner," she promised.

He walked back to the cab, youth in his step and a song in his heart. She stood upon the doorstep, watching him go until the cab was out of sight.

Then she turned to Mr. Willard. "Mr. Willard?" she asked, the question hanging between them.

But all he did was take her bags and smile. "Welcome home, ma'am."

Find out what happens next in Book Two - **Spirit of Denial!**

O'Hare House
Mystery Series

Book One - **A Spirited Manor** Book Two - **Spirit of Denial** Book Three - **Distilled Spirits** Book Four - **In High Spirits**

www.katedanley.com/ohare.html

Did you like what you just read?

P lease tell your friends and leave a kind review!

Sign up for the **Kate Danley Newsletter** to stay up to date on upcoming releases!

Links to all this good stuff and more can be found at **www.katedanley.com**

Author Bio

K ate Danley is a USA TODAY Bestselling author and twenty-five year veteran of stage and screen with a B.S. in theatre from Towson University. She was one of four students to be named a Maryland Distinguished Scholar in the Arts.

Her debut novel, *The Woodcutter* (published by 47North), was honored with the Garcia Award for the Best Fiction Book of the Year, 1st Place Fantasy Book in the Reader Views Literary Awards, and the winner of the Sci-Fi/Fantasy category in the Next Generation Indie Book Awards. Her book *Maggie for Hire* hit the USA Today Bestselling list as part of the boxed set *Magic After Dark*. *Queen Mab* was honored with the McDougall Previews Award for Best Fantasy Book of the Year and was named the 1st Place Fantasy Book in the Reader Views Reviewers Choice Awards.

Her plays have been produced internationally. *Building Madness*, a 1930s screwball comedy, won the prestigious Panowski Playwriting Award 2016. *Bureaucrazy* was a semi-finalist in the 2017 The O'Neill National Playwrights Conference. *Power* won Best of the Renegade Theatre Festival 2017. Her screenplay *Fairy Blood* won 1st Place in the Breckenridge Festival of Film Screenwriting Competition in the Action/Adventure Category and her screenplay *American Privateer* was a

2nd Round Choice in the Carl Sautter Memorial Screenwriting Competition. She is one of the founders of the Seattle Playwrights Salon.

Her scripts *The Playhouse, Dog Days, Sock Zombie, Super-Pout,* and *Sports Scents* can be seen in festivals and on the internet. She trained in on-camera puppetry with Mr. Snuffleupagus and recently played the head of a 20-foot dinosaur on an NBC pilot. She has over 300+ film, theatre, and television credits to her name.

She lost on Hollywood Squares.

http://www.katedanley.com